S0-BDO-671

Gardener Summer

Also by nova

American Apocalypse: The Collapse Begins
American Apocalypse: Wasteland

Gardener Summer

by

nova

Flying Turtles of Doom Press
Copyright © Steve Campbell 2011
All rights reserved, including the right to reproduce this book, or any portions thereof, in any form.
This novel is a work of fiction. Any references to real people, events, establishments, organizations or locales are intended to give the fiction a sense of reality and authenticity.

First published in 2010 by Flying Turtles of Doom Press in ebook format.
Previously published in unedited form online at http://theamericanapocalypse.blogspot.com.

Contact the author: stevcampbell@yahoo.com

ISBN-13: 978-1463662653

ISBN-10: 1463662653

First Paper Edition: July 2011

For Marilyn and Elizabeth

Acknowledgments

I would like to thank Bill McBride of the blog Calculated
Risk for his encouragement. Tanta Vive!
I would also like to thank everyone who read this story
online and left comments. Thank you very much.

Thank you to Chile, my editor. As usual you make it work.

Chapter One

Damn, I miss air conditioning. The power always seems to drop at night now. Probably because "They" figure it will be less disruptive. They are up to a lot of shit these days. Everyone knows it's "Them" but no one wants to say who They are. The furthest most people will go is to mumble something about the government. At least the people I talk or listen to. Then again, it isn't wise to badmouth the government too much. More and more that is something that is just not smart to do unless you know the people you're talking to, and as far as I am concerned, that limits me to talking to myself.

Why the fear?

Because They are spending a lot of media time talking about internal terrorism these days. And "They" don't like that the Burners are catching on.

The Burners aren't organized so much as they are a spontaneous reaction to how messed up the world is today. There is a guy who runs his mouth a lot, claiming to be their spokesperson. He writes a blog and even put out a book that is supposed to be like the bible. They also uploaded some hot videos of the group burning banks while the women danced topless.

Me? I don't give a shit one way or the other. My rule is just don't mess with me and everything will be fine. Anyway, the Burners aren't active where I live. Random violence is more of a threat than internal terrorism. Hell, from what I see and hear out on the streets as I go about my life, random violence is almost a daily occurrence.

Most of it goes unreported too. That is, unless you are valuable to "Them" or have enough cash to make it worthwhile for someone to look into. Around here, that eliminates all of us. We are in a gray zone. Close enough to the money that we can see it, but far enough away from it that we never get to touch it.

I sit up in my bed and avoid taking deep breaths. I smell, my room smells, and my boots, somewhere by the door, stink. It has been a while since deodorant sanitized my pits and I don't have a washing machine I can use for my clothes.

I hope to convince Night to let me use the motel one. It is going to cost me, though; this I know. Night is Chinese and, in my experience, the Chinese do not do anything for free. If they do, I haven't seen it around here.

Thinking about that reminds me that I need to make some money. It is only when I get down to the last bit of cash, or cash equivalent, that I get motivated. And I am getting motivated. I will think of something. I always do.

I take a shower and sniff-check the towel. It fails the sniff test. It has that sour smell that comes when you get something wet and it doesn't dry quickly. Jesus, I hate that smell. It reminds me of fat people, and I don't like fat people.

Actually I don't like anyone really. Carol, yes. Max, he is okay. Night is a pain in the ass most of the time. Her cousins, or brothers, or whatever the hell they are, qualify as annoying but are easily ignored. As far as I am concerned they are just a couple of Bruce Lee wannabes. In fact, as far as I am concerned, everyone else I run into on a daily basis just takes up space and resources, and is on the make for something.

I am supposed to be getting ready to head out. I'm scheduled to meet Max down by the Tree in fifteen minutes, which means I'll have to skip breakfast. He wants to talk about a business proposal and I want to be on time. He gets really pissy when I'm late.

His idea of being on time is arriving fifteen minutes early. My opinion is that if you want me to meet you at 08:45, then don't say 09:00. Just say 08:45. Sometimes I think his service in the military really messed with his mind. It doesn't help that I have problems remembering what military time, like 14:00, is in real time.

I need to brush my teeth. I attempt to do this but my toothbrush is a sad little thing. Most of the bristles have worn down or fallen out. It is rather mangy looking. I would love to replace it but toothbrushes are nowhere to be found; at least not new ones.

One of the vendors who is set up most days down at the Store offers a few gently used ones for sale. He tried to tell me they were new. When I asked why they didn't have boxes since they are new, he didn't have a good answer. What an asshole. I would rather brush with my mangy one than use someone else's almost-as-good-as-new-but-not-quite toothbrush. Toenail clippers are even harder to find. I really need a pair too. If I don't find one soon I'm going to have to trim my nails with my knife.

It is amazing how much of the stuff that we took for granted turned out to have been made in China. When they quit shipping because of the dollar default devaluation thing, a lot of stuff taken for granted just dried up, or is only available now at prices I can't afford.

When I finish brushing, I search for a t-shirt and a pair of pants that look clean enough to wear in public without attracting too many stares. I don't bother sniff-checking the socks; I already have from across the room. I slip my feet into my boots and take my gun belt off the hook it hangs on next to the bed. This is still a little strange for me - the whole gun belt thing. Max had a fit about my choice but I like it. I'm still not used to the weight but it feels right. So does the Ruger Vaquero .357 that sits in the holster.

Max taught me to never assume that it is loaded. Always check it every time I put it on. That, and clean it every night or after use if possible. I have found that I like cleaning it. It's also fun just to look at it. Sometimes I sit and spin the cylinder over and over. If I'm not doing that then I am practicing my draw.

I like to do that too. I am good and I know it. It is a strange feeling because I know this for certain. For the first time in my life, I have found something that completely clicks. With the Ruger hanging on my hip or in my hand I am complete. I also know that I will get even better with practice. Besides I don't have anything else to do.

There is a huge difference between where I had been before and the place where I lay my head now – a place that is sheltered and secure, has running water, and a flush toilet. Living in the woods was a constant struggle. Living in abandoned houses, hell, just sleeping in one, meant a low level of alertness had to constantly be maintained. Not that wandering around the streets in the daytime doesn't require the same thing, but the nights are better now.

I check the door to my room to make sure it locks behind me and start walking down the sidewalk to the road. It is cracking in places, and chicory and dandelions are coming up through the cracks.

I loved dandelions as a kid. They produced magical fluff balls that I could blow on, then watch as the seeds separated and floated away. A part of me enjoyed destroying those perfectly formed balls, while another part thrilled at watching the seeds float away, free and alone into the sky.

One of my Mom's friends, I don't think he had made it to "Uncle" status yet, caught me doing that and beat the crap out of me. He told me I was polluting the neighborhood and ruining the lawn. Like his fat ass ever stirred off the couch to do any yard work. I kept doing it, but it became a guilty pleasure.
After awhile I gave it up because it was no longer the same.

The Tree where I am meeting Max is close to the

women's shelter. It has become a place for men to sit and wait for their women to come out and talk to them. It has a bench seat from a car, some milk crates, and a couple of chairs that always seem to change. Someone comes by and adds a chair, and somebody else comes by and takes one. My guess is they probably drag them off into the woods to one of the Tree People camps.

The Tree is a big oak next to the "Store" down from the shelter. The Store is in a strip mall that is pretty much dead due to the fact that no one around here has any money to spend. All that remains is the old Dollar Store, and its shelves are mostly empty. The owners, a Korean family, stock some canned goods - usually dented, and occasionally milk and bread. You don't check the expiration dates on the bread, you check for mold. Most of their income came from selling lottery tickets and phone cards. The problem with getting power on a continuous basis also puts a serious crimp in selling anything that requires air conditioning. I haven't eaten ice cream in a long time.

Max is waiting for me. Supposedly he is teaching me advanced ass-kicking skills. So far I haven't seen much in the way of training from him, just a lot of talk. The guy is good at showing up unannounced in my room though. I put up with it because he comes highly recommended by Carol. I have been in love with Carol for years and now she runs the women's shelter. The Chinese people at the motel also think pretty highly of him. He seems kind of skinny to be a real ass-kicker type despite the fact he had been in the Marines.

He is standing next to the Tree, looking down the street at the usual group standing around in front of the empty 7-11. The shopping center is quiet. A couple of vendors usually set up there, in front of the empty nail salon and pizza place, to sell crap from shopping carts. Nobody is around today though.

"Hey, Max."

"Hey, Gardener."

He slowly turns around to face me, his face, as usual, expressionless. "Want to make some money?"

"Sure."

I purposely keep my voice unenthusiastic. Never let them know you need it. Never let them know you need anything. Period. "Who do I have to kill?"

"Well, cowboy, since we're going to clean up the town, I imagine you might get your chance. Carol tells me that if she doesn't pay some people money on a regular basis the shelter might get some visitors. Maybe some people might get hurt."

I think about that. I don't like that. I don't like that at all.

"You know who it is?"

"I got an idea where to start," he replies.

"Let's start then," I tell him. "Like right now."

"Not so fast. You have any idea what we are going to do?"

"No. I don't really care either."

Max gives me what passes for a smile, one that suggests *commendable attitude but not real smart.* Then he changes the subject.

"What can you tell me about the people hanging out on the corner down there?"

I flash back to the soup line when he asked me the same question about the people in line there. So I tell him, "None of them are carrying guns."

I think about it for a second and consider adding that they are a bunch of losers who love booze and drugs too much, but I bite that off. I am only one step away from living in the woods again myself. Who am I to judge?

Instead I say, "Probably some of them have a buzz going on or have some other issues."

"Do you know any names? Any of their back stories?"

"Yeah, Max. I don't see him, but one of the guys that

hangs out there used to work at my old company."

"The guy with the duct tape clothes?"

"Yeah, that's him."

"Find out about the rest. Find out about everyone around here. You need to know what names they go by and a little of their history."

"Okay." I don't see the point, or a reason to talk to any of them, but I agree anyway. It doesn't cost me anything.

"You see the white guy. Young. Long brown hair and tats?"

"Yep."

"I want to talk to him. While I do, I want you to watch my back. Don't shoot anyone unless you have to. This isn't Tombstone or Dodge yet." He pauses and looks at me.

"You got that?"

"I got it."

It makes me a little pissed too. I am not an idiot and I sure feel like I am being treated like one.

"All right. Let's go see how everyone feels this morning."

Chapter Two

We start walking towards them. I have a heightened awareness of the weight of the metal strapped to my leg and hip. The people don't seem too concerned by our approach.

There are four of them. Three are standing; one is sitting on an overturned empty white five-gallon paint bucket. My guess is that it is his personal bucket. Buckets are a sought after commodity. Much easier on your ass than a milk crate, and they come with a handle so you can load stuff in them and carry it much easier than in a plastic bag or milk crate. As we draw closer I wonder why they don't sit under the Tree. It would be a lot more comfortable. I am going to try and remember to ask Max later why that is.

We walk past the shelter and I wonder if Carol is there. I don't see her car in the parking lot but sometimes her husband drops her off.

Max tells me, casually, "Watch the black guy."

Since there is only one it is pretty easy to figure out which one he is talking about. He is a big guy. He and Long Hair are talking but turned so they can keep an eye on us. The fourth guy, middle-aged, white, and balding, turns and heads inside the 7-11. I don't know for sure, but it is beginning to dawn on me what the 7-11 is used for. Lately there has been an influx of decent quality, cheap Smooth. Smooth is a new designer drug that is a mix between ecstasy, THC, and some other chemistry goodies. Usually it makes the user feel good about whatever shape their life is in and about the world in general. It came out after I quit drugging so I missed out, once again, on the chance to feel good about my life. Not that it would work for me. That was one of the reasons I quit. Drugs promised a lot but the only thing they delivered was more pain. Law enforcement doesn't pay much attention to Smooth or the users. Then again, they don't pay much attention to anything anymore unless forced to. They are very unhappy about having their pay cut by 25 percent. Myself, I think they should be glad they still have a job.

We walk up to the guys that are still outside. Actually we walk a little past them, and then turn and come back to them.

Max says, "Hey."

I guess that covers everything because he gets a couple "Heys" back and the long-haired guy says, "Hey Max." That surprises me. Max knows this guy?

I also realize by the way they are squinting that we are now standing with the sun at our backs. It's still a few hours before noon but the light is strong and bright. I am delighted. It is just like in the books! We have the sun at our backs. Maybe Max does know a few things.

"C'mon, Tony. Take a walk with us," Max tells the longhaired one, who doesn't seem to understand that it really isn't a request..

"No, I don't think so." He doesn't sound real confident about saying no, though. I decide to let them know I am there too.

"Hey! Do what he says and nobody gets hurt."

It sounds good until it escapes my lips. Then it hangs there, a verbal dead fish stinking like a line from a bad cable movie.

When I say it I am standing about three paces from Max. The Black Guy is closer to me than Bucket Man. He laughs, repeats what I said in a falsetto voice, and laughs some more. I go cold. He looks over at Max, back at me, and asks, "This your new bitch, Max?"

I forget that I am armed. I forget everything. A wave of hate and anger punches like a fist up from my stomach and into my head. Before I can act though, Max is already moving. I notice the movement with my peripheral vision but I really don't see anything until his foot enters my narrowed frame of vision. His boot-clad foot connects with Black Guy's knee from the side and snaps it. The sound is literally like a stick breaking with a thin overlay of liquid tearing. I watch Black Guy's eyes widen while he topples like tree cut by a chainsaw. I hear Max tell someone, "Don't even think about running."

After the big man makes contact with the ground, I step up and drive my boot into his gut. I am not aiming or trying to hit pressure points or any of that shit. I don't know where they are anyway. I do know what it feels like to have someone take their boots to you when you are on the ground. I lay into him. He tries to go fetal on me. Fuck that. I kick him in the head and snap him back out of the curled position. I am getting ready to jump over him so I can work on the kidneys when someone grabs my arm in a vise grip. Max pulls me away from Black Man, telling me, "It's done. You're good." He keeps saying it over and over until he feels me relax.

I take a deep shuddering breath and say, "Okay. I'm fine."

He turns around to make sure Long Hair hasn't decided to relocate. When he does I kick the moaning big man in the chest and grin when he whimpers. Max doesn't even turn around. He just asks, "You done?"

"Yep."

"Draw your weapon. Check out the inside of the 7-11. I don't want any surprises. Then drag smart ass in there."

I move towards the hole that passes as a door with the Ruger in my hand. The plywood over the glass windows is covered with graffiti. None of it is understandable to me other than a faded pink pig stencil from some passing anarchist. I take a deep breath before going in. I know from experience that the first thing people do after breaking into an abandoned building is piss on a wall. I haven't been in one yet that doesn't smell like urine. Behind me I hear Max say, "Tony, you can start answering my questions anytime now."

I step in the doorway, exhale, and cautiously sniff the air. Hmmm.... not bad actually.

There is light. The storage room in back has been partially torn down and the door leading to the back is open. The cooler room is still intact, including the glass doors. One of them is open. The walls inside have the usual graffiti but the floor is only moderately trashy. A broom leans against the wall in the corner with an overflowing plastic trashcan next to it. Someone is making an attempt at keeping the place clean. A folding card table and two folding chairs sit in the middle, and a couch is against the far wall. I cautiously move towards the cooler and look inside. No one is home. A stained mattress lies on the floor, an unrolled sleeping bag on top of it.

I stick my head out the back door. Nothing there but a burned-out car and some weeds coming up through the cracks in the asphalt. Broken glass is everywhere. I have seen that before, a cheap alarm system that also discourages the barefoot and flip-flop wearers from passing through. There are a lot of those nowadays.

Bad footwear is starting to show up everywhere. America shod itself with cheap shoes for a long time. Now our supply of cheap shoes is gone and there are no more shoes to be had in America at an affordable price. Shoe factories, like almost every other factory we once had, were shuttered years ago and the workers let go. Outsourcing our manufacturing had worked out quite well, until it didn't anymore.

Now people's shoes are wearing out. In this part of town it isn't uncommon to see shoes held together with duct tape. The other day I heard, and then saw, the Duct Tape man. He must have found the mother lode of duct tape somewhere. He walks the streets shouting loudly over and over, "Duct Tape! Duct Tape! Get it here! By the inch or by the foot!" He seems to be doing all right too. Hell, my right boot has a seam that's tearing. If I can't come up with some real money soon I'll be buying a couple inches of tape myself.

I head out the front door and see that Max has his arm around Tony. Bucket Man is gone. So is his bucket. Max is listening and nodding his head to the nonstop stream of word regurgitation from Tony. Personally, I don't like getting that close to people as a rule. I'm not the only one brushing his teeth with a sad little excuse for a toothbrush.

I grab the Black Man by the ankles and drag him inside, hoping the leg Max kicked will come off in my hand as I do. No such luck. He does carry on like it has though. "Who's the bitch now?" I ask him. Then I let his legs drop, grin at him, and go back outside to find out what is up next.

I listen to Max tell Tony, "Thanks. Now go away." Tony doesn't hesitate. He is gone. I watch him until he is out of sight. Then I ask Max, "What's the deal anyway? Who would shake down a women and kids' shelter? I mean, there can't be any money in it." He laughs. "Sure there is. Not big numbers, but enough to make it worthwhile. Think about it. They run the clothes closet. A lot of that comes in free from the county collections. They could charge for it and the money could go into someone's pocket. Carol disburses the county debit cards each month. What if she, or more likely her successor, took 10% for bookkeeping?" I nod my head. It does make sense.

"Plus there are a few attractive ladies there..." He doesn't finish his sentence. He doesn't need to.

"So did Tony tell you anything?"

"Yeah. I got a name and address. We're going to go see him later on tonight. I don't think this a big deal. Just some small time guys with ambition."

"So where does our payday come into this?" I am curious. "We're not taking Carol's money for doing this, are we?"

Max looks surprised. "Hell no. Taking care of this is on

the house. It just happens to fit in with something else I'm working on."

I mull that over as we walk the couple blocks to the empty house Max decided to use for my training. For the next couple of hours, we go through the right way to enter a house, and how to approach a corner, a room, or a hallway. There is more to it than I thought there would be. Not a surprise. Everything I have found worth knowing so far in life has been a hell of a lot more complicated than it looked on the surface.

Before we go our separate ways Max tells me, "Be out in front of the motel at 03:00."

"That's the same as 3 o'clock in the morning? Right?"

"Yep."

Then he just walks away. Not big on goodbyes, I guess.

Chapter Three

I'm hungry, and I still haven't made any money. I make a right and head for the Store. About two blocks from there, the Taco Man is usually set up. I know it isn't beef in the taco. Probably squirrel, maybe dog. I don't really care. It's cheap and filling. Plus, I have found that if you put enough hot sauce on anything, it tastes just fine. I have one old time silver dollar left to my name. That should cover the special, a recycled Inca to wash it down, and a couple of tamales to go.

Taco Man pulls his taco cart behind his bike. He usually sets up off of Route 50 down near where Route 28 crosses it. I am pretty sure he comes out of the apartment complex across the highway. It is behind a thin crust of closed body shops and printers. The pawnshop there is still open; it does Western Union and will also give advances on government debit card payments.

I know the Taco Man's name. In my head I call him the Taco Man, but to his face I call him the same thing I hear his other customers call him: Jose.

I think he is all right. He looks like he has seen life from the outside more than a few times. I like that in a person; in fact I look for it. We usually talk if business is slow. Nothing of any importance but I look forward to it. I don't talk to a lot of people. My former means of conversation, my laptop, is dying so I try to use it frugally. I used to think I talked to a lot of people and had a lot of friends. I played a lot of HALO and talked to people there. I went a few other places online.

Sometimes I just lurked at Calculated Risk and read the comments. I never posted, but it still felt like I was involved in a conversation. Now I know that I wasn't. Virtual friends are not friends. When you unplug they are gone. You might as well strike up a friendship with an answering machine.

When I pay for my food, Taco Man looks at my silver dollar and chuckles. "You keep paying me in the good stuff and I am going to have to hire you to protect me."

"Okay," I say between mouthfuls. "Sounds good." He just shakes his head and grins. "So what did you do before this?" I am always curious about how people end up where they are, especially those who talk about how they had been Somebody until the bankers crashed the system. It makes me feel better about my going from a nobody to a nobody.

He looks surprised when I ask. I don't know if it is because I asked, or because he figured that I had assumed he was descended from a long line of taco sellers. He answers me quietly and with dignity. "I was a professor. A professor of literature at the Benemérita Universidad Autónoma de Pueblo." He says it like it meant something.

"So I guess that was pretty good?" He replies, "Very good. It was founded in 1587."

I am sort of stunned. I wasn't even aware Mexico had Universities, let alone that long ago. What did they teach? Landscaping? I thought they were living in stone houses cutting people's hearts out so it would rain back then. I want to ask him more but a Fairfax City police car eases into parking lot and stops next to us.

We both stiffen. One thing being homeless taught me right away was that the police had one face for the propertied class and another one for people like me. It later occurred to me that the face I saw was their real one since I posed no threat to their jobs. They are free to jerk people like me around all they want. What can we do about it?

Legal Aid is gone. The media? Do they even do news anymore?

The only good thing is they don't want to lock us up anymore. That costs money. What they do like to do is put your stuff in the trunk and you in the backseat. Then they drive to the city limits and kick your ass out. Who know what happens to your belongings. They probably are tossed out behind an empty office building after a quick look through.

Both officers get out of the vehicle, each one adjusting his duty belt almost identically. They might as well be clones. Big white males. Both around 6' 2", 200 lbs, and in shape. More than likely they are veterans from one of our country's losing causes. I have found the cops who are vets are a different bunch than the ones who have not served. Almost all of them are fair and polite. Where they differ is in their response when someone gets physical with them. The older cops still react like someone is filming them. The vets? They are getting a reputation as serious ass-kickers. It is like they don't care. Push their buttons and reap the consequences.

I am sure they are here for me. Don't ask me how I know that. I just do. I step away from Jose. No sense in him getting any of this on him. I figure it is about my kicking Black Man's ass this morning. It seems very unlikely, but it is the only thing I can think of. I am wrong.

They square off in front of me, maybe six feet apart Each one has his hand resting lightly on the butt of his Glock, ready to grip and go. It may not be perfect form, but it is a nice reminder of where they are willing to go if I push it. I keep my hand away from my gun, but I wonder … Hell, I know. I could take them if I wanted to. It is a cold feeling. I am positive, completely stone cold certain, I could do it. I can even see it happening in my head. Draw, head shot left. Head shot right.

I don't know what they see; perhaps it is standard procedure now, but the one on my right yells, "On your knees now! Hands behind your head. Lock 'em."

I obey. I don't want to, but I do. They change positions so one can cover me while his partner walks over to me. He reaches down, tries to pull the Ruger from the holster, realizes it has a rawhide lace loop holding it in, gets that undone, and eases it out. During all this he looks me in the eyes. He never looks down at his hand. I am impressed. I don't look away either. He walks backwards until he is about six feet away from me.

"Okay. Toss your identification over here."

I pull my driver's license out of my wallet and toss it to him. It falls short by a foot. He picks it up and goes back to their car.

"What's this about, Officer?" I ask the remaining one.

"Just a check, sir. Nothing to worry about."

"Can I drop my hands?"

"Yes."

This is good. If they wanted to jerk me around he would have said no. I look over at Jose. He has his back to us and is intently cleaning the side of his wagon. An old Buick passes by real slow so they can get a good gawk in. Minutes pass, then the officer gets out of the car and nods at his partner.

"He's good. You need to take a look at what he's carrying." He is holding my Ruger out so his partner can look at it.

"My God! A gate loader?"

"Yep. Single action. I've never seen one of these before."

"No shit. They were, like, state of the art a hundred years ago. Maybe longer."

They both laugh. The officer holding it continues to shake his head in amusement once they both are done laughing. He looks over at me and says, "You can get up." Then they go back to looking at my Ruger. While I am doing that, he adds, "Well, at least it's a Ruger." They look at each other and burst out laughing again.

I am starting to get pissed. I don't like them touching it to begin with. Disrespecting it like that is totally unnecessary. The cop holding it looks at me and says, "Come here." I go over and stand in front of them. He spins the cylinder, empties it on the ground, and then hands it back to me. He starts to say something, changes his mind, and they get in their vehicle. They roll out and I watch them go.

"Assholes," I mutter to myself and start picking up my brass.

"Yes, they are," agrees Jose, who is looking at me, a somber expression on his face. "Worse, they are fools." He spits to one side. I am so angry I am shaking. I don't want him to hear it in my voice and mistake it for fear, so I stay silent.

"I know that type of gun. My Grandfather had one. It is the weapon of a pistelero." He pauses, and then adds, "Your countrymen are fools. They always want the high tech guns. They don't understand. I think you do or will soon. A pistolero is one regardless of what he holds in his hand: a man not to be trifled with."

I just look at him.

"I go now. Maybe never come back. Stupid country."

He mutters the last as he settles on his seat. He pushes off, gives a brief wave, and pedals off without looking back. *He better come back*, I think as I watch him go. He still owes me some tamales, at the very least. I burp and wipe my lips off with the back of my hand. Goddamn, I like Mexican food.

I head back to the motel. I consider going by the shelter to see if Carol feels like company. Nah; she is usually busy. She is polite about it but it still stings. I am not in the mood for rejection or feeling like a loser. What just happened did not do anything for my ego as it is. Instead I decide to go back to my room and clean my gun. Maybe practice some more. Maybe practice a whole lot more. Which is what I do. I run through the cop stop two hundred times in my head. Visualize, draw, dry fire, and then back to the holster.

I get lost in the robotic motion of it all. It isn't tiring. It isn't boring. It is the closest thing I have found to meditation and inner peace.

Chapter Four

I only stop practicing because I am hungry again. I have soup and rice rights along with the room. Well, it's mostly soup. I am sure Night and her crew eat better elsewhere, but the soup is always there to feed anyone who shows up. It fulfills the family's duty to be hospitable and, from my daily sampling, it doesn't cost them a lot to offer it. Not that I ever complain. It beats the alternative, which is having nothing to eat.

I figure I will eat, maybe play some HALO, take a shower, and then go to bed early. To wake me up, I have a cheap windup alarm clock that has tripled in value since I bought it out of a vendor cart three months ago.

Vendor carts are somewhat new. I think of them as mini mobile yard sales. They contributed to the recent policy of grocery stores locking down their carts tighter than most of their customers do their cars. Each vendor is unique, and each neighborhood has a different range of merchandise for sale. There are even franchises.

It is kind of funny, and sad, that some people consider selling goods, mostly secondhand, out of a stolen grocery cart to be a good job. I figure it is only a matter of time before the independents get run out of business. The clans and gangs will eventually end up controlling all of them.

Some of the vendors sell food, usually canned goods past the expiration date or broken up cases of food stolen off a truck. Some sell clothes. Others sell housewares. They are beginning to congregate at the dead strip shopping centers. I guess pushing those carts burns more calories than they make. Might as well be stationary since the police no longer run them off. Being run off by the police was why they went cart mobile in the first place. Early on they couldn't stay put for long without getting moved on.

No one is in the motel break room so I sit down on the sofa and drink my soup rather than use a spoon. It is less messy that way and easier to clean up. Today's soup is basically broth with carrots and a bit of rice. It's not too hard to drink when there is hardly anything to it.

I really miss bread. It's strange what I miss when I can't afford to buy food. It never stays the same either. Sometimes I crave steak. One time it was canned sardines. I learned to go into McDonald's and take the salt packets during the summer. Living outside and sweating a lot I had to, otherwise I would cramp up. While not my favorite meal, I used to pump a bunch of McDonald's ketchup into a container and then mix it with water. Add a little heat and I had tomato soup. They got wise to people doing that, though, and moved all the condiments behind the order counter.

After my soup, I planned to log in to one of the computers that sits in the break room, surf the 'Net, maybe play HALO online for a bit. Instead I find myself sitting on the sofa staring at a screen saver. I feel uneasy. About what I don't know so I decide to go back to my room. As I walk in the door I check the clock. It is still early, plus I don't feel like going to sleep. Instead I unbuckle my gun belt and add a hunting knife to my pants' belt, and then strap the Ruger back on. I slip the knife in and out of the sheath three times for good luck. I am ready, but I don't know for what. I think I'll go down to the Store, see what's up, and then sit under the Tree and watch the world go by. I can keep an eye on the shelter and the corner from there too. Hey, who knows? Maybe Carol will drive by and wave. I laugh at myself and think, *How lame can you be?* It may sound lame but that is the way it is. It has been that way for a long time.

I stand there looking at myself in the mirror for a minute while I think about her. It is unrequited love.

That is what I have specialized in for most of my life. There were exceptions of course. I usually didn't love them though. It was easier that way. My life, such as it is, has been a mixture of chaos, poverty, abuse, and cartoons. When I got older I added alcohol and drugs, which only made things worse in a different way. I got over those and met my ex-girlfriend in a Narcotics Anonymous meeting back when I had a job and an apartment. When the job and apartment disappeared, she did too.

I've loved Carol since I first saw her when I was a sophomore in high school. Nothing ever came of it. My life was shattering and I was halfway to being a barely functioning vegetable. I was emotionally shut down and desperately wanting to feel better. She went on with her life. I hung around a bit and ran off to explore the world. If I hadn't, I probably would have killed my latest "Uncle" and, who knows, maybe Mom too. I shake my head at my reflection, laugh, and head out. I shut the door behind me, and check to make sure it locks.

I've only taken three steps when one of the Ninjas - I never can keep straight which one is which - comes running around the corner from the front of the motel. The little dude is flying across the concrete towards me and screaming my name. "Gardener! Gardener!" He comes to a stop in front of me. He isn't breathing hard. He and his brother, or cousin or whatever the hell he is, stay in pretty good shape.

"Come quick! Some guys are at the shelter. They're hurting Carol!"

He starts to say something else but I don't hear it. I am already running. Running is an understatement. I am flying. I can hear junior Ninja's worn sneakers beating the pavement behind me. It is downhill most of the way, and then it levels off as I turn onto the street. I can see the shelter in the distance.

Carol is standing near the fire exit that faces the street I am on now. The fire exit is close to her office, and she uses it to slip out and have a quick cigarette sometimes. A car is parked on the sidewalk, and three men are standing around her. One of them is waving a handgun around. When I am about 100 yards out I slow down until I am moving at a fast walk. I don't want to be breathing hard, let alone blowing wind, when I get there.

I study them as I approach. The one waving the gun is talking shit to Carol. The other two are watching me. I can't read the eyes of one of them because he is wearing sunglasses. He has a handgun tucked into his waistband. I can't tell where the other one's weapon is. That means he probably has it covered up by his shirt

A voice behind me asks, "Why did you stop running?" I had forgotten about the little idiot. I growl, "Get your ass out of here, kid." I can't turn around to look at him because I don't want to take my eyes off the men as I approach. I tell him to get Max. After a second's hesitation, he runs off. It would be good to see Max now, but I know this is going to be decided in the next few minutes. Hell, I am going to make sure of that.

By now I am close enough that everyone focuses on me. Good. That is the way I want it. I look at Carol. She is pissed and scared at the same time. Rather, she had been angry but it is draining out of her now and being replaced by pale white fear. It makes her green eyes stand out nicely. I wink at her.

"Hi, Carol. How you doing?" She nods her head, opens her mouth to say hi or something like that back but nothing comes out. I stop. I am a little less than fifteen feet away now. I stare at the guy waving the pistol around like he is a star in his own personal video. Great, another Scarface fan.

"What's up, guys?" They look at me like I am an alien from another planet. After a second, Gun Waver laughs and says, "What's up? What the fuck looks like is up? Get your ass back to cowboy land." He laughs again. His crew laughs. He turns to look at them, probably checking to see that they appreciate his wit. The gun he is holding at shoulder height moves with him and off of Carol. I draw and shoot him in the head.

I am using factory standard .357 jacketed hollow points. As I fire, a jet of flame shoots out the barrel. I like that. I compensate for the kick, re-cock the hammer and shoot the guy next to him in the throat. No fire this time from the barrel sadly. He had been moving; going for the gun he had tucked in his waistband. The throat shot sends a jet of blood almost as impressive as the flame from the first shot. The third guy is slow. Way too slow. He has his hand underneath his shirt, reaching for his weapon, but he doesn't have a chance. I look in his eyes, and he knows it just as well as I do. In the background I hear Carol shout "No!" but it is too late. In that fraction of a second where neither one of us speaks to the other, we have a conversation just standing there, staring at each other.

His eyes say, "Fuck! I'm beat." Then, "Don't do it!"
Mine reply, "Tough shit."
His acknowledge with "Oh God." Then I shoot him. It is done.

Off to my left I hear Carol say "Oh Jesus" in a voice both sad and horrified. I want to tell her that Jesus doesn't listen to us anymore. At least he never listened to me when I was a kid and called out to him to stop the pain and insanity. I look at the bodies stretched out in front of us. I take a couple steps forward for a better look. Messy. Other than that I don't feel anything.

"Oh my God!" One of Carol's coworkers has come around the corner. "Carol! Are you okay?"
I look at Carol. She looks at me. There is nothing there in her eyes for me other than horror and disbelief. I look away. She comes out of her shock enough to start thinking. "Gardener. Go back to the motel! Now. I will take of this." She asks her coworker, "Did anyone call 911?"
"Yeah. I did," she - I think her name is Darlene - replies.

"Okay. Go inside and lock us down. Then come back here." She looks at me and says, "Just go." She softens her voice and adds, "Please."

I leave, cutting sideways across from the shelter and through the back of an empty plumbing parts store. The trail I take from there runs parallel to a creek. Following that takes me two blocks north of the motel. The motel is built on the slope of a hill. I take a branch of the trail that leads up the hill and find a place to sit in a patch of pines and boxwood. I can see the shelter easily from here. I settle down to see what happens while a couple of crows let everyone know where I am. I reload and wait.

Fifteen minutes pass since Darlene said she called 911. Still no response. They will get one eventually. They are a county-funded facility for homeless woman and children, and the potential media problems outweigh the increasingly lethargic response time. It doesn't help that the shelter is one block into the county's jurisdiction and one block out of the city's. Each police force will try and lay the slow response off on the other.

It isn't that they aren't good cops. There just aren't enough of them anymore. The politics of budget cuts also determine where they patrol. The county funds its services primarily through collecting tax revenues from individuals and businesses. Every purchase by an individual is taxed, and all property is taxed. When people started losing jobs, they quit buy anything more than they had to. Nice hit to the county money tree there. When their homes got foreclosed, or they just quit paying the mortgage, the money tree lost another branch. Eventually the county had to start cutting services. They began at the outside; parks, libraries, and literacy programs went first. Then they started working towards the core. There had once been six county shelters. Now there is only one – Carol's.

The unemployment numbers peaked and stuck there. Eventually the county started cutting emergency services. It is common knowledge that if you live in a neighborhood with a significant number of foreclosures, you will not get the same response as you will if you live in a "good" neighborhood. This is not a good neighborhood.

After 22 minutes the first county police car shows up. An unmarked car is right behind it. I watch them get out, look at the bodies, and then start talking to Carol. I am glad they finally showed up. She must have smoked her week's ration of tobacco waiting for them. An ambulance shows up five minutes later. That is the total response. A few years ago there would have been twenty units on the scene. A helicopter would have been buzzing around and a couple satellite masts would have grown out of the roofs of the media vans. Not anymore. This is the new world.

I can't say I am that impressed by the response. I find it depressing actually. I am not going back to my room right away. I am pretty sure Carol has my back but not enough to risk taking a chance on the American justice system. My desire to avoid the justice system is based on stories I've heard on the street. Nowadays it is hard to get locked up for any length of time. If you do, it is hell. I have already been to hell. I can do it again; I'm just not going to make it easy for them this time.

I figure Max will get word of what happened. Our 03:00 mission will have to wait. I am pretty sure it will be canceled anyway due to lack of live bodies. My guess is the people I met in the street were the same ones trying to shake down the shelter for protection money.

Chapter Five

I decide to fade from view for a couple days. Maybe more. It means living in the Land of the Tree People but I'm okay with that. If one is going to live in the woods it is better to do it with other people. That way there are always eyeballs on your gear. More people out scrounging also means more chances of someone finding something good.

The problem is finding the right group of people. I stayed with a decent group for a while not far from here. The question is how many are still there and if the group has changed for the worse since I last saw them. Not all who live in the woods are damaged. The ones that are damaged usually stay to themselves or flock to like minded groups. Some groups just provide a place to do your drugs, chase it with alcohol, and sleep. Others have a dominant male who runs the group like a fiefdom. Some are becoming clans, usually specializing in petty theft or some sort of scam. Some bounce back and forth between squatting in abandoned houses and living in the woods.

The one I lived in briefly had a medieval renaissance festival meets the new millennium and is transformed into a bunch of acorn-gathering political activists theme. It had a lot of low level IT people. About the time I left, some of them had brought in enough cash to rent a small house. They were talking about using it as a place to shower and wash clothes for the group. I left because the politics were getting a little intense for me. Hopefully though they are still around. If not I will make do.

The sun is starting to set so I pick up my pace. The group I am looking for has people who were early arrivals to the woods and they had gotten one of the better sites. It wasn't deep in the woods, not that you can go all that deep because of the building that had happened around here. It was a choice spot because it was in the woods next to a business campus that never reached more than 10% occupancy at its peak. That gave us some privacy. The main benefits were the pond that had been built for scenic value and the paved trails throughout the campus.

The pond was great. For a while ducks and geese used it. That didn't last too long as they were very good to eat. In the summer the pond provided water to wash up in, and, when purified, drinking water. It was the result of a man made hole scooped in the ground and then filled by a dam across one of the many creeks that ran through the area.

The Tree People community tried to protect the water from dumping and from random idiots using it as a toilet. They succeeded only partially then because they relied upon reasoning with offenders. As I pass the pond now, I can tell they eventually failed completely. I can see the top of a minivan stuck in the middle of the pond. That had to have taken determination on someone's part

I find the right trail and within minutes I know there is not going to be a homecoming. They are gone. *Well, that sucks,* I think. It is time for Plan B. That sucks even more. Plan B means hitting up one of the Fundie shelters for a blanket. No way in hell I am going to stay in one. That is for fresh fish and frightened families. The costs are too high. Not in money; in having to listen to the sermons. That, and they are the watering holes of the worst type of predators.

To get anything of substance from a Fundie shelter you have to go to the rail during the call. Get down on your knees in front of everyone and accept their version of Jesus into your heart. I know a few people who are professionals at getting redeemed. Then they "backslide" and come back again seeking forgiveness. Usually the shelters wise up and cut them off after the third or fourth time, but there is always another shelter or someone else who just has to help them down the road somewhere.

I am going to miss the start of the dinner seating because I will get there too late. At best I will be at the end of a long line, which means getting the dregs of whatever is being served. I laugh to myself. I've gotten spoiled. Not all that long ago, even the dregs would have been worth waiting for.

At least it isn't freezing cold. It has been a mild winter and spring already feels warmer than usual. I cut back through the campus and walk on the side of the main road that runs through it. It is usually dead from what I remember but at least two cars pass me. That's unusual. The streetlights actually work here too, at least the ones that are not burnt out yet.

Up ahead I see a young girl come out of the woods and stand under one of the lights. She is dressed for August at the beach. *Damn,* I think, *the meat trade has made it here too.* Prostitution is not a big deal to me. I never worked it but I understand the motivation. Being hungry is a bitch. The drug of choice for people working the streets is Smooth, although anything that numbs you is probably a winner.

I say "Hi" as I walk past her. She ignores me. I'm not a client and she sure she doesn't want me hanging around talking to her. It will just scare off the Johns. She is young, maybe fourteen or fifteen. There are two more like her not far away, hanging back, right on the edge of the bushes that have grown up to the side of the road. I know there is a path through them with the entrance only a foot or two away. Like rabbits, they always try to have a bolt hole.

I keep walking. I pull out my shirt so it covers most of my holstered Ruger. There is a chance that a cop might see it, consider it concealed, and stop me on that, but it is safer than hanging it out there, especially if they are looking for someone with a holstered revolver like mine.

I pass a couple of young guys standing on the other side. Something for everyone.

Foreclosures and living in cars is hell on family life. It had been my experience, even in the best of times, that stable families were rare around here. I wonder how many of these kids end up in basements or dragged into the woods to rot. More than a few is my guess.

A black Honda Hybrid Civic passes me, taking its time as it goes by. I'm sure I'm being scoped out. I decide to cross the road. Up ahead is a short cut that leads between two buildings. I'll lose whoever is in the car. I really am not in the mood for leering old men.

Whoever it is sees me cross the road. They speed up a bit and make a U-turn so they can pull up alongside me. I slow down, and look over as the window rolls down. It isn't him, but he is close enough in appearance to be my old high school government teacher. He had been a Republican, Jesus-loving asshole. It figures that his clone is out here looking for love.

He smiles brightly and says, "Hi! You're new here, aren't you?" Then his gaze drops to my crotch. He looks back up to smile at me. It is a wide smile. A friendly smile. A rapidly disintegrating smile. I stop walking and he stops his car. I am left-handed so my holster is on my other side. The one he should have seen earlier. I guess he wasn't looking in the right place.

I draw and pivot as I do, swinging the Ruger around in an arc at waist height. It connects with his face, exactly where Mr. Smiley has his ivories out for display. It snaps his head back and teeth come popping out of his mouth like kernels of corn. It is awesome, so I do it again. He has his hands over his face the second time so I get to break a few fingers. Bonus points.

Then I holster the Ruger and drag him out the open window. He is a skinny old fart. I drop him on the ground. Without his foot on the brake his car begins rolling away. I let it. I am pretty sure the car stereo is playing something by the Beatles as it does. He is moaning. I let him moan. I reach in his back pocket and pull out his wallet.

Then I kick him once in the ribs and head for my short cut.

Once I get off the road and onto the trail I stop to take a look inside the wallet. It takes me all of ten seconds to realize it is a roller. He probably had his real wallet hidden somewhere inside his car. This one has his license in case he was stopped, and enough new dollars to pay for what he was looking for. Since there is a glut of willing orifices on the market it doesn't hold a lot of money. Still, ten dollars, even if it is in new dollars, will come in handy.

Do I hate gay people? No. I do hate assholes that use the fact that they have money to buy the services of the young. Especially when these assholes portray themselves as righteous Christians and family men in public. I don't know if he fit the first part but I had seen a wedding band when his hands came up to cover his face.

I walk away without looking back. Did he live? I don't know. I don't really care. I don't even think of it as a big deal. Callous? Perhaps. I know no other way. I realized I was different early in my life. One of the main differences between most people and me is they live in a world where they expect a beginning, middle, and end to any event in their life. Me? Shit just happens. I got a dog. The dog disappeared. "Uncle" Bob came out of Mom's bedroom, said good morning to me like he had for the past three months, went off to work and never came back. One day I was living in a house and going to school. Two days later I was living in another town and going to another school. I never knew why and I quit asking. Stuff just happened.

All I know and care about right now is that I have a Plan B. I have only partially figured out what Plan B entails other than hitting up the Fundies. Other than that all I can think of is to clear the area, so I head out. This path is well used. In the woods it is the equivalent of a two-lane highway. I don't see anyone else on the short stretch where I am walking. I hear some movement off to my right in the bushes at one point. I draw the Ruger and pull the hammer back.

It clicks on its way back and the noise in the bushes settles down. This is one of the reasons I like the Ruger. It talks to me with an audible click for each stage it goes through as the hammer is being pulled back. The final click is it telling me in Rugerish, "I'm ready!"

I come off the trail where it feeds into a dead end street. There is a car parked there and I give it a wide berth. It has curtains in the windows and etiquette is to give them some room if you can. This is called the "Texas" rule. Supposedly it is the result of a court ruling in Texas that said a man's car, if being lived in, is his home. That means he has the right to defend it and a radius of seven feet around it. This has become part of the vocabulary, as in "Step away from my car or I'm going to go Texas upside your head."

I don't know how they came up with seven feet as the magic number. Maybe because people in most Car People communities try to keep an empty parking space on all sides of them. It gives them a place to set up their chairs and coolers, with room for the kids to play.

This one has suitcases underneath it. Not unusual. People keep their suitcases in the car until they need the space. Then they take them out and slide them under the car. Sometimes they tie them to the wheel. Sometimes, in a good Car People community, they don't need to. I am surprised to see a car like this alone. Usually, if they are at the stage where they have put up curtains, then they are in a community. Safety in numbers and all that. I keep going and forget about it.

I walk up from the dead end until I reach the corner of the street. While I do, I work on Plan B in my head. I need a blanket to roll up in for sleeping, and a free dinner. That means the Fundie soup kitchen. I also need to rent a phone to find out what is going on. Then I need to kill some time hanging out for a bit before I go looking for a place to sleep. Maybe I can find out what happened to the people I knew from the Tree People camp that disappeared.

Chapter Six

I head for the Fundie soup kitchen. I have been to this one before. I am really glad it has been awhile since my last visit. When they first opened, I hoped they would have a cross with a neon "Jesus Saves" on the roof like I've seen in the movies and in old photos. No such luck. Apparently there are laws against that sort of tasteless use of neon. Might make property values go down or something.
They should have let them do it. It would be a lot prettier than the people the place attracts, and a hell of lot classier than the ones that run it. Jesus knows I hate those assholes. They know it too. They either ignore it, or they glory in it. I guess they confuse my hatred for their pompous, smug, self-satisfied, narrow-minded, lying asses with a hatred for the god they serve. I don't have a problem with Jesus, just with those who use his name to further their own personal twisted hatred and agendas.

I get there barely in time for dinner. I am just stepping in line behind a woman and her kid as the End of the Line marker man is making his way towards us to seal the line off. The Ender wears a phosphorescent yellow vest like he is working on a road crew. On the back is stenciled:

"END OF LINE
NO
EXSEPTIONS."

I tried pointing out a while back that it was misspelled and the Ender wearing it told me, "That's nice. Jesus loves you." I tried again and got as far as "But it's..." before she had smiled sweetly at me and told me, "Shut the fuck up.

Jesus loves you." They say that a lot around here, especially the "Jesus loves you" part, although they usually say the "Shut the fuck up" part with more passion.

The kid in front of me is maybe five. She alternates between hugging her Mom's leg and letting go of it to see what is happening up ahead in the line. She never goes far, at best a foot or two. Not because Mom is paying attention. Rather, it is because she is genuinely shy but still interested in what the world has going on. I make faces at her and listen to this end of the conversation her Mom is having on her cell phone.

"What do you mean you didn't get the car?"

"What? I gave you enough money."

"You said..."

"You son of a bitch. What am I supposed to do now?"

"Well, fuck you too!"

She snaps the phone shut and moves forward cursing. The little kid peers up at her with a worried face.

"Mommy?"

"Not now, honey."

I see her Mom's shoulders shaking and know she is crying. "Mommy..." the little girl says tentatively and holds up her arms to be picked up. "Not now!" Mom snarls and pops the phone open again. She must have him on speed dial because she is snapping it shut again a handful of seconds later. By then we are at the door.

The kid and her Mom pass through security. The kid looks back at me and I wave goodbye. She gives me a smile and a little kid wave. The security guy just gives me a bored look. "Check the weapon and move through. Hurry up. We're closing in fifteen."

To my right a young lady sits at a table; the shelf behind her holds a couple of handguns and hunting knives. The woman in front of me with the kid does not make the turn this direction so she is clean. I am not the only one who notices that.

There are a scattering of single guys, a couple, and a

family still finishing up their meal. I notice two of the single guys tracking the woman and kid. They aren't together, as far as I can tell, except maybe in what they are thinking. They see me un-holster the Ruger and hand it over in exchange for a claim ticket. They watch me for a couple of seconds before they go back to looking around the room. Still no eye contact between them. Interesting.

I am passed through security after turning over my gun and emptying my pockets. I stuff everything back in and am stopped again on the other side by the tract man. He hands me a tract, which I keep. They are just the right size and with three pages are perfect for toilet paper.
He asks me, "Will you accept Jesus into your heart?"

"Not today."

"Jesus loves you."

"Great."

Now I am free to get my food. I have wondered a few times what would happen if I said, "Yes! Gimme Jesus!" Would bells and alarms go off? Would balloons appear? Would the water-stained ceiling panels drop open and confetti rain magically down on me? Best of all would he shout, "Winner! Winner! Chicken dinner!"? I am not going to find out tonight that's for sure. Instead I grab my metal tray with the indentations for food built into it, and slide it down the steel tube rail in front of the steam trays.

Mom and her kid have gotten their food already. She is standing there, at the end of the serving line, looking for a place to sit that feels safe and gives her enough space. I see one of the men who had been watching smile broadly at her and indicate with his hand that they are welcome to sit with him. She ignores him and goes to sit in the middle near the family that is finishing up. As she does I get to see her from the front rather than the side or back. It confirms what I thought; she is not bad-looking.

Her skin is still good. Women who spend a lot of time outside are easily distinguished from those who don't. Those who have a choice have their tennis for toning and poolside tans that have been buffed and oiled by lotions; their time spent under the real sun is carefully limited. Homeless women's tans are not enhanced by spray guns. Homeless women usually end up looking like models from the Dorothea Lange agency. Even freshly washed and shampooed, they are easy to pick out with skin that has been overexposed to the sun and shows every blast of its rays.

Her hair is its natural color, a reddish brown, which makes her a bit of a freak also. Bleached blond is the color of choice for the high-end homeless woman. Her body is good, not a lot of fat, she is clean, and her clothes are neat. Her appearance screams "Fresh Meat."

My guess, based on the phone conversation, is that tonight is the first night on the streets for her and the kid. She probably has fallen from the ranks of the Car People. Based on the way she looks, and the cell phone conversation, she hadn't spent much time on that ledge before continuing the tumble down. Although, from the phone conversation, it sounds like she may have been pushed.

The meal tonight is spaghetti with tomato sauce. The same has been served every time I have come here. There had been garlic bread to go with it but they ran out before I got in. I am disappointed. I like garlic bread.

I take a seat a couple tables at an angle behind the woman and kid. I am not interested in watching her as much I want to watch the watchers. The kid eats everything on her tray in less than five minutes. I notice her Mom gives her half of what is on her plate without making a big deal of it. She just smiles at the kid, and - it isn't hard for me to read her lips - tells her, "I'm not hungry." The kid doesn't catch the lie but I do.

Tract Man starts walking the tables and yelling, "Five minutes! Five minutes to closing!" I see the woman motion him over. I know what she is asking. Is there any room at the inn? He shakes his head. I ate faster than the girl so I am ready to go. When I walk past them, I hear Tract Man telling her to try the County Shelter for Women and Children. Better known, at least to me, as Carol's Place.

I leave my tray at the window and go to pick up my gun. One of the two watchers is ahead of me. The other is lingering over his meal. The guy in front of me is in his late twenties, white, needs a shave, and is wearing a Steelers tshirt and a windbreaker that he puts on before he get his gun back. I don't like him and I don't like the Steelers either. He picks up a snub-nosed .38, slips it into his windbreaker pocket, and leaves.

The only weapons left beside mine are the hunting knives, and a small automatic of some sort. Two knives for one man? Interesting. I pick up my gun, smile and nod when I am told, yet again, that Jesus loves me. I cross the street quickly and cut across the parking lot of a used tire store. Once I get across the lot I break into a jog, run around the building and up the street a bit before stopping. I now have a clear view of the exit at the mission.

Windbreaker Man has walked about twenty feet from the exit and is taking his time lighting a cigarette. The other watcher, a short stocky Hispanic guy who looks to be in his thirties clears the door, hesitates, and does a quick scan of the street, including the Steeler lover, and crosses the street like I had. The woman and child are right behind him. They are still talking to Tract Man as he hands her a piece of paper. I recognize it. It is the shelter flyer and it has a map on it. He points her in the right direction and goes back inside. She hesitates, takes a deep breath, takes the kid's hand and begins walking. She doesn't know it, but it is now show time.

I have no idea what I am going to do next. I mean other than kill one, or both, of the watchers should it prove necessary. I am not going to be getting a blanket tonight. Maybe I can still work the phone in. No big deal. I can always join a fire circle.

Fire circles are our brave new age's answer to fire

barrels. There are established ones and ad hoc ones. The established ones attract certain types of people. None of them are the type you would want to spend any time with during daylight. These have chairs and places to lie down and they generally want something in return for letting you be close to the fire. Usually you kick in a bottle or a blunt. Generally, if you don't have anything to contribute, you can sit or stand in the second row. You won't freeze, and you will be drinking dregs, but it is better than nothing. I spent a few nights that way early on.

The woman I am watching would automatically get a good seat. It would come with strings attached but that is the way it is. Most of the good fire pits have a Tender or two. They keep the fire going, make sure there is enough wood for the night, and hire a Head Knocker to keep things from getting too crazy. Those are the best ones. Sometimes they even have potatoes you can buy and cook in the fire pit. They are also great places to hear the latest gossip and news.

While I am running all this through my mind Windbreaker Man makes his move. He lets her get about twenty feet away from the Fundie mission. This is a good sign. She is still in hollering distance. It might not matter, but then again Tract Man might want to play hero. Windbreaker Man will know this too. That tells me he is going to go for verbal rather than physical persuasion, at least at this point. I watch as he hails her, then hustles up to her grinning. I am too far away to hear his pitch, but it is pretty easy to guess what script he is using. It probably goes something like this:

Windbreaker: "Hi, looks like you might need some help?" A cheesy grin quickly followed by, "I might be able to help."

She recoils a bit, and instinctively pulls the kid in closer.

Windbreaker: "Whoa! I am not going to hurt you."
He raises his hands to show his harmlessness. "Hey. Cute
kid. What's your name?" He bends over a bit.

The kid hides behind Mom's leg.
"Shy, huh? I have, well, had, a kid like that." He
switches to a sad face. "Say, look …" This would be said
brightly, and then followed with the close.
She is already shaking her head, she isn't buying his sales
pitch, and she is walking away. *Wrong way*, I think. *Go back
to the kitchen, woman.* No. She has a map and a plan. She is
going to the shelter. I watch him. I know he just said that he
could walk with her. She is shaking her head no. Now she
turns away and starts walking faster. He watches her go and
yells "Bitch!" at her back. She doesn't turn around.

Chapter Seven

I imagine I can hear her heart beating from here. The kid looks up at her, and then back at the man. She is worried. Her Mom snaps something at her and jerks her arm to hurry up. Windbreaker Man watches for a minute, shakes his head, and turns. He is walking in the opposite direction. Good. One down. Now I need to hurry up. I am going to try and parallel her and still keep the remaining watcher in sight. He is going to make a move. I know this. I don't know how I know this. I just do.

The woman and child are still walking fast. They are scared. Somewhere over towards Oakton I hear gunfire. That is not uncommon. What is uncommon is hearing sirens afterward as the police respond to it. I don't hear any sirens tonight.

When I first hit the street I didn't know what gunfire was when I heard it. I used to think it was firecrackers or trucks backfiring. It was just inconceivable to me that people were actually firing weapons here. Downtown, sure. Out here in suburbia? No way. Well, it is that way. It isn't always at people. The deer population is being thinned out rapidly. The first time I actually heard a gun fired, it was fortunately not being fired at me. I just happened to be in the wrong place at the wrong time. The guy who ended up bleeding to death in the street less than fifty yards away probably thought the same thing. I didn't understand what the hell was whizzing by my head. I thought it was bumblebees or something. It wasn't.

I was lucky that I was standing around listening to some older guys talk shit amongst themselves. Probably about the coming One World government. That was real popular then. Two of them were vets. One second they were standing up. The next they were flat on the ground. One of them cut my legs out from under me and took me down right after the bumblebees went by. I would have thanked him once I figured it out but I never saw him again.

I am moving but I've lost sight of the woman, her kid, and the second watcher. I get hit with an adrenalin rush. "Jesus! Get your shit together!" I mentally yell at myself. I burst into a run and come out behind them. Watcher Man is maybe fifty feet in front of me. The woman and kid are about a hundred feet in front of him.

He looks back. I know he feels me but I am frozen in place next to a tree. I look away from him to minimize his ability to sense me. He starts moving, then abruptly stops and turns around. I haven't moved. I knew he was going to try something like that. I would have.

I am running my mental map of the area through my head. If I was him, where would I take them? There are a couple of good places. My guess is about a block and a half ahead where the road passes a wooded area. They will be on the sidewalk next to it. The woods start about two feet from the sidewalk.

I cut back over to the next street and run like my boots have wings. I want to get ahead of everyone, across the street, and enter the woods first. I cross about a block ahead of the woman and child.

I notice that Watcher Man is closing the distance between them. They are aware of him but she can't go any faster. The kid's legs are too short. I don't just casually cross the street; I keep running at an angle. Let them think I am jogging, or running from my own demons.

I make it. I hang a sharp left and enter the woods from the side opposite of their approach. Every clump of trees around here has a path running through or by it. This clump is about as deep as the yard for one of the older houses and maybe twice as wide. It was probably a lot intended for a couple of McMansions that never got built.

I tell myself, "Okay, find where the path comes in from the sidewalk side." I start pushing through the clump. "Ow! Shit! Damn thorn bushes." I can hear the kid's voice so I freeze.

"Mommy, that man is getting closer!"
Mommy answers, "I know, honey. Come on. Let Mommy carry you. We are going to play Mommy runs like a pony." They are almost even with the entrance to the path. She stops to gather the kid up into her arms when he hits them.

The woman is taken completely by surprise. So am I. I expected him to be a little more subtle. He hits them at a run, wraps them both up in his arms, and flies into the woods. He goes airborne as he does, and when they land, he is on top. They are stunned and I hear the woman's breath go out of her with the impact. I also hear the kid cry out.

The asshole does a one-arm pushup on top of her. The other hand is holding his blade. He has nice white teeth. I'm glad he grins because now I know exactly where his head is.

I come out of the thorn bushes like a startled bird stopping only to set my legs. He turns his head to see what the hell is happening. It's a bitch to get up fast when you are balancing your upper body on one arm and the other hand is full. He has to make a decision quickly: respond to me or hold the woman hostage. He doesn't make a decision. He doesn't have enough time. He has other problems. Mainly me, and I make the decision for him.

I kick him in the head; right in the ear to be exact. You cannot imagine how good that makes me feel. His head snaps hard left and I see blood spring instantly to the surface of his skin. The earring he is wearing glints in the moonlight, just like the blade of his knife.

He shakes his head and snarls. I kick him again, almost in the same place. The fucker moves on me though. He rolls to his left as my foot connects, and then he's up like he has springs inside him. His face is lopsided. We stand there for a microsecond facing each other. I suppose I should be worried. This guy is in good shape - really good shape. I'm not worried though. Instead I feel good. So good I laugh from pure joy. I see a flicker of doubt in his eyes when I laugh. His are dead eyes, just like a snake's. I know snake eyes. I used to stare into them in their cages at PetsMart Snake staring contests. I usually won.

He is moving his blade slowly in front of him. I draw the Ruger and shoot him dead center in the chest twice. The barrel flash is blinding in the darkness. He goes backwards, slowly stumbling back out towards the trail entrance to sprawl next to the sidewalk.

"Fuck," I swear. I holster the Ruger and go after him, grabbing his ankles to drag him back into the woods. The blood from both exit wounds stains the grass black in the moonlight.

I drop his feet and turn around. The woman is still lying there, holding the kid tight to her chest.

"Hi. You want to get up?"

She doesn't move. She nods her head, but her eyes are too wide, and she looks a little pale. She doesn't look like she is processing what I just said very well.

I try a different tact. "There may be more. They like kids, you know." That gets through to her as I hoped it might. You can't have been one of the Car People and not have heard the stories.

"You shot him." It is a statement of amazement rather than a question.

"Yep." I laugh. She looks at me like I am crazy. "Oh, I was thinking, you know...that old saying..." She shakes her head. She isn't following me. "You know. Never bring a knife to a gunfight." I laugh again, and start going through his pockets.

"He was going to rape me," she says shakily.

"Yep. And that was probably just a warm up."

I hear "Mommy" and then "Ssshhh. Everything is

going to be okay."

I pull out his wallet. He has three new ten-dollar bills. I think, *Damn. I could make a living at this.* I find the automatic, the extra knife, and a set of keys. That is interesting. I pull his ID out of his wallet. Unfortunately nothing in his wallet shows an address.

I toss the keys, along with the wallet, over my shoulder into the thorn bushes. I pat him down to his shoes and find nothing else. I straighten up just as she moves next to me. She kicks him hard twice.

"Feel better?" I ask her.

"No." She stares at him, and then kicks him again. She looks up at me and hisses, "Men are such assholes." Not a lot I can say to that. "Oops. Almost missed something." I step forward and rip the earring out of his ear. "Okay. Now we are set." The little girl says, "Yuck," and giggles. I look at her, and then hold the earring out to her in the palm of my hand. "You want it?" She looks up at Mom for approval. I watch as different responses form and then disappear. She nods her head, and I drop it into the kid's hand. "For good luck," I tell her. She smiles and clenches it tight in her hand. I hand the woman one of the ten-dollar bills and tell her we need to move. We leave the woods without looking back.

We walk side by side. Just like we are out for a stroll. "Nice night," I tell her. She looks at me, rolls her eyes, and then laughs quietly to herself. Both the kid and I look at her. She catches it out of the corner of her eye, shakes her head, opens her mouth to say something, and then changes her mind. I mentally shrug. I know I really suck at small talk, especially with women.

I look down at the kid who is walking between us. "You okay, kiddo?" She smiles at me shyly and says, "I think so." We walk another block in silence. Then the woman says, "I'm sorry. I wasn't laughing at you a minute ago. It's just ... it's just so weird. You know ... all this ... and what happened. I still don't think I believe it."

"Yeah, I know. When you get to the shelter you might want to keep it to yourself."

"No shit," she replies. "Look." She stops walking, which means I stop too.

"I'm sorry. I haven't even thanked you. Jesus, you saved our lives, and here I am acting like a bitch." She reaches out and touches my arm. "How can I repay you?" I read the message that is there. I am not totally clueless. My brain is shrieking, "Get some head! Get some head!" I tell her, "Don't worry about it."

"You sure? I mean..."

"Yeah." I shrug. "Maybe you could let me use your phone?"

"Ah ... sure."

She pulls it out. Had I seen disappointment? I sure hope so. We start walking again. She is studying the map while I flip the phone open and stare at the keypad. I realize I don't know anyone's phone number. That is a very strange feeling. I snap it shut and hand it back to her.
She takes it and asks, "Changed your mind?"

"Yep."
We walk quietly for five minutes. She breaks the silence telling me, "I think we are almost there." She's right. I can see the shelter at the end of the street.

It's time for me to go. I realize I do want to go. I don't want to go back to the shelter or the hotel. Not yet. Hell, I am enjoying myself. I feel free. "Yeah. That's it." I point to the building. "I'll stand here and watch until you get in." She is disappointed. "This is it? Just like that?"

"Yep." I add, "Maybe I can come by and see you sometime?"

She gives me a big grin. "Of course!" Then she stands up on her tiptoes and kisses me real quick. "You better." She takes off. The kid looks back at me, waves, and says, "Good bye." I wave back and watch from the shadows until I see them go inside. She looks back but I am already gone.

Chapter Eight

I need a room for the night. I find it in an industrial complex of one and two story buildings. The complex once held a high percentage of granite and tile distributors, office furniture warehouses, and printer service shops. Now it holds a high percentage of vacancies.

The Motel is in a five-story office building that had once been a Korean real estate company and probably a few other things before that. The real estate company has their name, Star Realty, in English and Korean on the front of the building in big letters. The sign is still there, but the neon lights up just the first four letters "STAR" in the night.

I walk in through the main doors, which puts me right in the lobby. They have a doorman by the door although I don't think that is his job description. He doesn't open the door for me. Instead he just gives me a quick scan with eyeballs that are probably more efficient than the x-ray machines at the airport. I must pass because he goes back to watching the almost nonexistent traffic on Route 50.

Only a couple cars are parked in the front lot. That doesn't mean anything. There is plenty of parking, including a multi-level parking garage attached to the building. The lobby is clean, and a fit-looking Asian man in his late forties occupies the concierge desk.

The lobby has a small waiting area off to one side furnished with a couple of sofas and a table. An older Asian man is sitting there reading an Asian paper and smoking a cigarette. He looks at me when I come in for a little bit longer than necessary.

The concierge says, "Welcome to the Hotel Star, sir. Can

I help you?"

"Yes. I would like a room. Do you have a rate sheet?"

"Certainly, sir." He hands it to me. While I study the rate sheet, which looks like it comes from the same printer that did the Chinese food menus I used to get in the mail, he studies me. He does not look impressed. I mentally sigh. Prices have gone up. Well, at least it has a nice lobby. The rate sheet is in Korean and English. A large portion has not been translated but I see dollar signs. It would not surprise me if there are two sets of prices. Possibly three, with the third not written on the menu. I can afford it, but I am not going to walk out of here tomorrow with more than six or seven dollars, at best, in my pocket.

That's when the old man yells something in Korean at the desk clerk. He looks surprised. The old man yells something again, and he gives him a tiny bow in acknowledgment of whatever the hell was just said. He takes the menu out of my hands and says, "Sorry. Old menu. We have a new price for you tonight. Five dollar. Full service." I look at him. "Why is that?"

"Special."

"Oh. Okay." I shrug. Something isn't right, but I don't feel any weirdness or wrongness in the flow around me.

"Any chance I can get a toothbrush and toothpaste?" I hastily add, "a new toothbrush."

"No toothbrushes." He shrugs. "Toothpaste okay."

I decide to see what else is in stock. "How about a gym bag or backpack?" He looks up at the ceiling, then at his nails, and finally at me. "Okay sure. I can do that. Anything else?"

"No. I'm good. How much?"
He waves his hand. "For you, Mr. Special, nothing. You have Room 3, 2nd floor." I head towards the elevators. He calls out, "No elevator. Take the stairs please."

I walk up the stairs. They are clean and don't smell like piss. *Curiouser and curiouser*, I think. *A first class establishment, this Hotel Star.* I exit the stairway at the second floor and enter a wide hallway. At the far end a young Asian guy sits behind a metal desk. I ignore him.

My room is an actual room. The company probably used to have the standard layout of offices along the windows, and cubes in the center. My room isn't the corner office, which would have been bigger, but it isn't bad, especially for a "Special." I shut the door, and slide the bolt. If someone wants in bad enough they will only be mildly inconvenienced by the bolt. It will still give me time to greet them. That is all I need.

The room is what I expect. Instead of a dresser there is a desk and office chair for furniture. The bed is the usual concrete blocks with two hollow panel doors lying on top. Very nice; a twin bed. I always like a little room to stretch out.

I sit in the office chair, set the Ruger on the desk, and wait for my supplies to arrive. It took them about fifteen minutes, which is amazingly quick. I got up to answer the knock and am surprised to see a moderately attractive Asian woman in her early twenties with Sharpie eyebrows. "I have your sheets and the items you requested, sir." I let her in. She drops the sheets, a pillow, and a thin blanket on the desk. On top of the stack are a backpack and a half used roll of toothpaste.

"Thank you." I hand her a new dollar as a tip. She takes it and stands there smiling at me. I stare at her quizzically. She gets to the point. "You want the special?" Everything is special at the Hotel Star tonight it appears. "No, thank you. You're very attractive, but I think I will pass." She doesn't seem very disappointed.

"Okay."

She lets herself out. I watch her go with some regret. She has a nice ass. I like to tell myself it is a matter of principle that I don't pay for sex. If I were honest, it is because I am perpetually broke. It just makes me feel better sometimes to think I have principles.

I make the bed and then go in search of the bathroom. It is down the hall to the right. I brush my teeth using my finger and the toothpaste. One of the stalls has been converted to a shower. It is in use by a couple. Both are male it sounds like. I sigh, decide to pass on using the shower, and go back to my room.

My backpack is a kid's school day pack with Optimus Prime on the front. That is cool. I stretch out on the bed and begin thinking about what I want to do tomorrow. I get as far as "buy some socks" before I fall asleep.

I wake up early. I went to bed early, as I am accustomed to doing. I got into that habit early on. Most of the charities that disperse goodies do it early in the morning, so if you are staying in a shelter that is when it is time to get up and get out. Another reason to avoid shelters is not the early rising as much as the resulting stampede for the inadequate bathroom facilities. I had slept well. It was a quiet night. The working girls must have another floor to themselves. I stretch and look over to see Max sitting in my one chair, his feet propped up on the desk.

"Good morning. I thought you knew you are supposed to jam the door with the chair when sleeping in a strange motel."

"It's a hotel, Max."
I am pissed. Pissed because I missed his entrance, and because he is right.

"True. Let's go." He stands up, yawns, and scratches himself. "I was getting sleepy watching you. Come on. I'll buy you breakfast and tell you about the fabulous money-making deal I worked out for us."

"You know you are lucky I didn't shoot you," I tell him. "Yeah." He lets it go at that. I grab my boots and lace them up. Max passes me my daypack. "Optimus Prime. Hmmm ... Hello Kitty sold out again?"

"Fuck you, Max."

We hit the stairs a few minutes later and come out through the fire doors into the lobby. Max stops in front of an Asian lady who has a table set up with a chafing dish for spring rolls and two pump thermoses with coffee and tea. He says something to her in Korean, probably "Good Morning," and indicates by pointing that he wants enough rolls and coffee for two. She grins, says something incomprehensible back, and gives him six rolls on a piece of printer paper that she pulls from a copier ream. "You need to get your own coffee," he tells me over his shoulder. He does a little bow; she does a deeper one. We get our coffee. As we pass the concierge desk, which is now run by a young man, he bows. The doorman does also. I know they aren't acknowledging me or my egg rolls.

"So, Max. You come here a lot?" I ask once we get out the door. "I live here," he tells me before stuffing most of an egg roll in his mouth. "Let me guess. The breakfast is free here to guests?" He winks, and reaches for another egg roll. *Okay*, I think, *that's the way the egg rolls.*

I can never stay mad at Max. Hell, he barely irritates me at best. Probably because I never sense any malice or cruelty directed at me personally. If I sensed that, I would probably shoot him, or at least try to. When that thought crosses my mind, there is a niggling doubt that he is the only person for whom I might not be fast enough. I am beginning to realize that maybe, just maybe, I have found something that not only am I good at, but that I might actually be world class at. It is exciting, calming, and scary, all at the same time. Scary because I grew up listening to how worthless I was. It is exciting to know I am not. Calming? Liberating might be a better word. I no longer live with the fear in the back of my head of when or from whom the next beat down is going to come.

I grew up fearing drunken "Uncles." Then Detox told me I was powerless. The process of becoming homeless had further proven how powerless I was. Discovering Mr. Ruger changed all of that. By how much, I am only beginning to grasp.

Chapter Nine

It is going to be a beautiful morning. The azaleas are starting to bloom and the sun feels good on my face. Spend any amount of time being homeless and you will find yourself becoming in tune with the weather. Just like for the farmers, a string of rainy days can be a disaster. An unexpected early freeze is usually fatal to someone. The weather, when it is good like this, is my friend, and I welcome it.

Max finishes chewing the last roll and says, "Let's take a seat and talk a bit." The seat he indicates is the concrete lip of a flower box that once held professional landscaping. Now it holds young weeds and a dirty rag that was once been part of a Hawaiian shirt.

"You are clear on the shelter action."

I nod and say, "Okay." I don't feel relieved. I actually don't feel anything. It is already starting to feel like ancient history.

"Yeah. It was written off as a gang killing." He shrugs.

No surprise there. Fairfax City has zero homicide investigators, and the county only has four to handle a caseload that never stops dying.

He continues, "They thought they might have a witness but he disappeared last night." He says it casually, but I understand what is being said."I owe you." I say it as a statement. He answers as if it had been spoken as a question. "Nope."

We sit there in silence for a bit. Drink some coffee, and watch a homeless couple come out of the bushes by the parking garage. The coffee kicks in, and I start getting antsy.

"So what's the moneymaker?"

He grins. "Killing wannabe Nazis and assorted believers of Jesus."

"Okay."

Killing Nazis, Republicans, Socialists, Unitarians, or members of Elk Lodge 312; it doesn't matter to me. Someone unarmed I might balk at. Kids? That isn't going to happen, but somebody sporting an attitude and a weapon is fair game.

"You want to know more?" I think I notice a hint of sarcasm in his voice.

"Sure."

Max sighs, looks away, and scratches his nose. "Try to pretend like you care, Gardener. You look better to other people when you do."

"Right. I got it." I do too. It's probably in that book I never got.

He starts saying, "The Chinese who own this place ..." I interrupt him. "I thought they were Korean?"

"No. The Chinese provide the money. The Koreans run it. The Koreans pay the Chinese a percentage of what they make."

"Sounds like a sweet deal."

"Yeah. The Koreans are not all that thrilled about it, but there is some other stuff involved that I am not sure I want to understand."

I nod my head like I have a clue. I do know how to pretend that fairly well I think.

"You don't have a clue about what I am talking about, do you?"

"No," I reply. Why lie?

"Okay. Well, keep pretending. It will make this go faster.

The short version is the Chinese traded weapons for other merchandise with these wannabe Christian Nazi dickheads. The merchandise turned out to be lacking and they want some payback. They, for political reasons, would prefer it to be non-Chinese doing the payback."

"So where are these dickheads?" I ask.

"I don't know, but I know where to start looking. You know anything about the Christian Identity Movement?"

I shake my head.

"Aryan Nation?"

"Yeah. I've heard of them."

"Here is an easy one. The Christian Independence Movement?"

He's right. That's an easy one. The soup kitchen is affiliated with them. Along with the Catholics, a few other churches, and the County, they do a lot of outreach to people who need help. These groups are the local safety net, and in that order.

I had heard about them, probably starting the day I hit the streets. If you give yourself to Jesus, they will take care of you. They provide housing and feed you. Actually, they require you to live in their group housing. In turn you work for the "community." If you have a job, then your paycheck goes to them. It sounds good at first, especially the security in belonging. It is scary out here for the new fish, especially those who have never known, other than through music videos and Grand Theft Auto, what this other world is like.

The reality, at least what I have heard, is plywood bunk beds, working your ass off, and lots of Jesus teachings. Their version of Jesus, that is. No sex between the worker bees is allowed. Well, it can be done, but it is tricky. Shawn, a friend of mine who tried it for a couple weeks, called it "The Jesus Army for White People." They aren't 100% white. Maybe 99.5% - the Asian I saw with them had dyed her hair blond.

They are nationwide and popping up all over the place. The worse the Great Recession gets, the more they grow. Local governments love them. They feed people, and keep them busy at no cost to the government. They have a couple of charismatic leaders. One is a rather hot-looking cougar.

They are, last I heard, going for third party status with a national slate aimed at low level, local elected positions and targeted congressional districts. People like them and their message. As best as I can figure it out, the message is "God loves America. We are being punished for wandering from our values. We will be great again. We have the map that leads to that greatness. Join us, and be a part of it. The few, the humble, the Christian."

It has its appeal, just not to me. I am not fond of Jesus pushers for a lot of reasons. I'm also not a joiner. So I tell Max, "Yeah, I've heard of them."

"Good, because they use the local Christian Identity people as their action arm. I need you to spend some time with them."

"Doing what?" I am a little skeptical about this.

"I need some names to match with names I already have. Plus, I want your impression of them."
"Why does this sound like I'm going to be doing this alone?"

"Because you are."

He continues, "I know, but I can't do this part with you. They know me, and they don't like me."

"Why? You fuck someone's wife?"

I am pissed about being sent off alone and just reaching for buttons to push. His eyes narrow for a second, then he tells me, "You really can be an asshole sometimes. No. Because they know I do the occasional job for the Chinese. Just because they love Jesus does not mean they are idiots."

"Will I be able to keep my Ruger?"

"I don't know."

Not the reply I want to hear. I think about it, mentally shrug, and tell him, "I'll do it up to the point they want me to give it up. Then I'm gone."

"Fine. I'll give you an address to start at, and a number to call me if you need to.

You sure you're okay with this?"

"Yeah. Just make sure Night doesn't lock me out of my room." Max laughs. "Yeah. I'll talk to her. You can go back anytime you want now, you know." I think about it, and then tell him, "Maybe I will. Maybe I won't. At least for now."

"Yeah, well, just stay away from the 'Star.' These people are not stupid. If you get anywhere with them, they will do their own version of a background check."

"I got it, Max." I look at the address. "I guess you aren't going to drop me off near there, are you?"

"Nope."

"That's what I thought."

We stare at each other for a few beats. I'm ready to go, but I know I am supposed to say something. Something like "Roger Wilco," or manly and confident. I can't think of anything. Max solves my dilemma for me. He stands up, slaps me on the shoulder, says, "Don't be an asshole," and walks off. I watch him disappear into the parking garage and sit there for a while enjoying the sun. The woman who offered me the "Special" last night walks out of the building and past me. I call out "Morning" and smile at her. She ignores me and keeps on going. I sigh and decide to go find the address.

Once upon a time the idea of walking to get somewhere, especially an address that I estimate to be at least three miles from where I am sitting, would have been inconceivable. Now it seems as reasonable as walking from my cubicle to the parking lot had once been. My bike would make it a breeze. I think about going back to the Anchorage Motel to get it, and maybe even taking a shower and changing my clothes. But my feet are already moving in the opposite direction, and I have never been big on turning around once I get going. Plus the bike would just be something else to keep track of and make sure was always secure. That feels like more effort than I want to deal with today.

The shower? I don't stink that badly and it gives me the street guy cred I might need. Smelling of soap and freshly shaved, at least with these people, would give the wrong impression.

I had discovered that I like walking. I learned that telling yourself you know an area or neighborhood because you drive through it is a lie. Walking through a neighborhood gives it another dimension, sometimes more than one. You get the smells, and find the trails and shortcuts. You get the rhythm of the people that live and work there. It makes you sharper.

Being homeless, or just walking through the same places I had once driven, made me grow an extra antenna for sensing the "flow" of a place for lack of a better word. People become more real to you if you physically pass them repeatedly on foot over a period of time. Real in a way you never feel from inside a car with the iPod pumping out sound through the car sound system. If anything, I had begun to look at people in the cars that pass by as prey: fat, stupid cows protected only by their metal skins.

One of the disadvantages of walking as your primary mode of transportation though is that your world shrinks. I remember reading that for a thousand years most Europeans never went more than twenty miles from where they were born. I thought, when I read that, that they must have been a timid bunch. Now I am starting to understand why they didn't travel far.

Today I am heading into areas I rarely travel in. I usually go towards DC rather than away from it. The address is at the far edge of my world; it is where the subdivisions and open spaces start. You have to walk too much for too little out there. Being homeless out there makes having a bike a necessity. The good news is that it is safer. The bad news is it is also easier to go hungry because of the scarcity and distance between food banks and missions. I am not a big fan of being hungry.

To get there, I have to cross the Desert. That is what I

call this section of Fairfax on my mental map. The Desert is almost all asphalt so it is always hotter or colder than everywhere else.

Once it was lined with car dealerships, fast food and bad food restaurants, medium box party stores, and pet emporiums. Now it is full of sun-faded "For Lease" signs in unwashed windows. The empty parking lots radiate the sun's heat. Roving bands of grinning middle-aged Asian women who will eat anything harvest the chicory that struggles to come up through the cracking asphalt.

I wish I had brought water. Water - drinkable water – is always a major pain in the ass to come by. I can hit the residential areas with my empty bottles and fill them from an occupied house with an outside tap. Better than paying money for it.

At least the DC area isn't like Los Angeles where water shortages are getting to be a big deal. Here, we have streams. The only problem is if you drink from them, and you did not grow up in Lagos or Ethiopia, you are going to hate life for a long time. So for now, I go thirsty. It's not the first time, and I am sure it won't be the last time either. Traffic on Route 50, which runs through the middle of the Desert, is light. It is rush hour, although that doesn't mean much anymore. The bulk of the traffic is federal government employees and people working for companies hanging on the government teat.

Gas is expensive. Everything you need is expensive, and the stuff you don't need is expensive too. Expensive if you don't have a job. If you are still working, and not sweating the possibility of becoming unemployed, then life can be good. At least that is what I hear. I don't know where this place is where life is good like that. Maybe Oregon or Wyoming.

I take a shortcut behind a shopping strip and see a couple guys trying to lower pieces of an A/C unit onto a flatbed. I doubt if they are there to fix it. They have a tripod rigged up with a pulley on the roof and are moving the pieces that way. It looks like hard work. I pass one of them standing next to the cab of the truck. He is yelling at them to get their shit together. As I pass him, I say, "Hey." He replies without taking his eyes off the guys on the roof. Life is like that around here nowadays.

Chapter Ten

My address looks like it is going to be in a light industrial section on the edge of the Desert. There are a lot of those along this section of Route 50 because of the proximity to two Interstates and the urban core of DC. The only growth industry in them is leasing empty buildings to ministries and churches. I guess empty light industrial buildings make great starter cathedrals. Probably light on the stained glass windows but granite altar tops should be easy enough to find.

I find the building, but it is not what I expect. I would not have been surprised to see a hanging tree out front with the effigy of the week dangling at the end of the rope. Not do they have a flag pole with the Stars and Stripes flapping in the wind and their banner right below it.

Even the handful of cars and trucks parked in front are nondescript. The bumper stickers attached to them are the only sign that the drivers are special. I think the faded one that shows Obama sitting in a big pot on a fire with the caption "Cannibals Are Starving In Africa. Send Obama To Help" is very tasteful. The "In Case Of *Rapture* This Car Will Be Unmanned" sticker puzzles me. At first glance, I think it says, "In Case Of *Rupture* This Car Will Be Unmanned." I figure getting ruptured would be unmanning, but what does that have to do with anything? Then I realize it says "Rapture."

I know about that. God is going to call his special children up to him. They will rise up into the sky and go directly to heaven. I've always wondered what would happen if the person next to me started floating away and I grabbed onto their feet. Would I get to go too? Or would God flick me off like a booger? Maybe, if I can't think of anything to say when I get inside, I can bring that up.

Inside turns out to be as nondescript, at least at first glance, as the outside. I walk into what is just another low end office reception area from everywhere and anywhere. Industrial-grade carpeting. Molded plastic chairs. A side table with pamphlets. They even have a receptionist behind a desk.

She is blond, of course. Not naturally, also of course, and big breasted, probably not naturally, but still, of course. My first thought after contemplating her breast size is that I'd like to find out whether they are natural or not. After she smiles at me though, that thought is replaced with "Eek! Danger! Recovering meth head."

When I walk in an alarm must have been triggered automatically or by the receptionist because a young, white, bald guy comes out and stands there watching me. He is armed with the standard, black "operator" holster rig that is so popular with the cool kids. He is wearing a plain white tshirt and a pair of faded desert camo BDUs bloused into his black Doc Martins. He doesn't say anything. He just goes to parade rest and stares at me.

The receptionist asks, "Can I help you?"

"Yes. Do you have any water?"

He is unfazed by my request and answers for her.

"No. Can I help you?"

"Well, the water would be a nice start." I see her look impatiently at Baldie, then back at me. She sighs, and says slowly and almost clearly, "We have no water. We are not a shelter."

I hold up my hand. Partially to stop Baldie from making the move I know he is waiting to make. The other reason is to cut her off before she sics him on me.

"Okay. No water. That is not why I am here anyways." I pause. The problem with making stuff up as you go along is that sometimes the words, well, they just aren't there. Out of the corner of my eye I see someone else appear next to Baldie. I have to say something.

"I'm here to join the Army of God!" Then I add, "I'd really like a Dr. Pepper if you have one."

Blondie stares at me, her eyes narrowed, and then she says, "Zeke. Help me out here."

Baldie moves and so do I. I time it perfectly I have to say. I really impress myself with the fluidity of my draw and how the barrel ends up resting against his forehead exactly where I want it to be. I have the hammer back just a tiny bit behind the actual centering of the barrel between his eyes. The clicks as the Ruger goes to full cock sound good too. I am going to have to work on the synchronized thumb movement, but all in all it is damn near perfect.

Baldie's eyes cross for a second, and then he begins giving me the death stare. I grin at him and say, "Zeke. Come on. You got to admit that was a sweet move." All I get in response is "Fuck you."

The nice thing is I can see the other guy better now. Without breaking eye contact with Zeke, I shift a little to my left so I have him framed clearer. He is a Zeke clone with an extra 50 pounds and ten years. He is also bald. I hate it when white men do that. It makes them all look alike. Like a bunch of shiny penis heads.

Then Blondie, who I can't see, has to go and ruin it. She racks a shotgun. Even though this is the first time I have ever heard it in real life, the sound is distinctive. Pretty damn close to what it sounds like in an online game.

Zeke smiles at me. I smile back. After a second or hour or whatever the hell amount of time passes, his eyes change. He knows what I know. I am going to pull the trigger anyway.

Big Zeke sees it too. He says, unnecessarily loud it seems to me, "Tammy! Safe it." A pause. "Do it! Put it down, Tammy." It occurs to me that Little Zeke is probably dicking her.

"Okay," Big Zeke tells us, "let's all settle down and take a deep breath here. Son, I want you to take two steps back towards me." Zeke does, and I let him go.

I move a bit more to my left until I am facing all three. I still have the gun pointed at Little Zeke. I see no sign of the shotgun but I can tell Tammy is pissed. She probably isn't going to get me that Dr. Pepper.

Big Zeke says, "Okay. Let's start over. You want to holster the six gun, buddy?"

I almost said no but I realize that I am fast enough that it won't make any difference at this point. So I do. The mood in the room changes, and I realize everything that just happened was a choreographed dance as structured as anything a troupe might have done a few years ago.

"Thank you." Big Zeke tells me, "I came in at the bit where you said you wanted to serve in the Army of God." He pauses, and I watch his face change. Big Zeke is a subtle thinker. He probably really sucks at poker. "Damn. You were the guy at the shelter the other day! You're the cowboy." He doesn't say it as a question. He sounds excited about it.

I almost say yes and then realize that would be more than a little stupid. Instead I say, "That was a gang thing." Then I grin at him. He catches on. Big Zeke is sharp. "Right." He grins back. "That was good. Protecting the women and ridding the city of some worthless trash." He is nodding his head in approval. Big Zeke and me are halfway to being BFFs.

"So you want to be in the Army of God?"

"Sure."

"Come on back. Let's talk about it. Tammy, get the man something to drink."

He heads down the hallway and I follow him. I don't feel the love when I brush past Little Zeke.

We keep going past what I am sure is his office and into a small conference room. He sits down and gestures expansively to the empty chairs. "Have a seat. Rest your feet." He thinks that is pretty funny. When he gets done laughing he sticks out his hand. "Pastor Isaiah Brown." I shake it and tell him my name.

"So, Gardener, tell me about yourself," he says once we both have settled in.

I give him a brief overview. It goes like this: "I had a job. The job went away. The money went away. Everything else followed it. I have been living on the street since." He is a good listener. About halfway through we stop for a minute so I can thank Tammy for the bottle of water she brings me. It is cold and good. I drain it, and go back to my sad tale of woe. I don't lie, and it doesn't take long either. When I finish he just nods. Then he says, "So are you churched?" That's a code word I know. "I'm okay with Jesus." He isn't sure how to take that but he decides to let it slide.

"Well, I would say you're welcome to attend services here but that might not be a good idea. The FBI likes to pay attention to my flock. We don't have any pretty girls for you either." He sounds sad about that. I decide to tweak him a bit.

"Well, there is Tammy."

He looks at me sharply, and then says, "Yeah. Well, she can gobble like the pro she was but she is taken at the moment." Now it is my turn to look sad.

"I can offer you a job as a monitor at one of the Christian Independent Movement's houses. We help them out sometimes." He is watching me. I am sure he thinks he is a pro at reading faces, but I started my schooling at the University of Pain at a very early age. I know how to fake the emotion I think appropriate to the occasion or go stone-faced.

"That sounds good, Pastor." I pause. "What does it pay?"

That is the right answer. He laughs. "Not much. You get food, board and 25 new dollars a week."

"Great. When do I start?"

"I'm going to need you to do some paperwork. You don't have any W's out do you?"

"Not to my knowledge." Which is true. I don't have any warrants out that I know of.

"No child support? None of that shit?"

"No, sir."

"Okay. We are going to need to scan your fingerprints and get your social. You wouldn't believe some of the government mandated hoops we have to jump through. You can do that with Tammy. She will give you the address of the house too."

Chapter Eleven

"Before you go I would like us to say a little prayer."
He bows his head. I sit up a little straighter and bow mine.
"You go ahead, Gardener," he tells me. *Lovely*, I think, my
mind searching for any fragment of remembered prayer. Too
bad I never learned any formal ones. I have heard a few over
the years, especially at the Fundie places. I tried praying as a
kid but gave up when they were answered with nothing
except more pain. I don't like pain. Well, when in doubt, roll
the bullshit out.

"Dear Lord. Help us to be to the best we can be. Let
us reap the harvest, sow the seeds, and drive the tractor of the
Lord down the rows. May we kick the asses of the evil
ones, splatter their heads like ripe pumpkins, and kick their
sorry asses into the fiery pit. Let us pluck their eyeballs out.
If they cry, well, let us mock them for being pussies. Let us
kick their shiny white teeth..."

I stop and look up. The Pastor is looking at me. He
seems a little disconcerted. I smile at him. He looks away for
a second, then back at me and says, "I got it from here." He
finishes up with a mix of the usual platitudes and some
bullshit about being White warriors against the hordes of the
Antichrist. His final line is "...and may Yahweh smite the
mongrel offspring of the white banker whores who lead our
country. Amen."

I know I am supposed to chime in with a loud
"Amen" here but I don't feel like it. I am also pissed about
being interrupted. I felt like I was just starting to roll. So I go
back to praying.

"Oh yes. Smite all the assholes. Make them burn! Rip

them! Gut them, Sweet Jesus!" My voice is rising. I am getting into this. I am also starting to feel like ripping the head off this bald-headed, traitorous, lecherous piece of shit sitting next to me. Hell, I want to kill them all. I stand up.

"Kill them, Lord. Kill them all!"

The words are starting to come faster. I can't keep up with them. I throw my head back, and scream. Part of me thinks, *Whoa. Stop it. Stop it now!* Another part is saying "Oh yeah! This feels good!"

The Pastor is up. I can hear him telling me to calm down. That's when a pair of arms wrap themselves tightly around me from behind while the Pastor tells me, "It's okay. It's okay."

I go cold and rigid. I know I could flip whoever has me from behind. I see just how to do it. How, after I flip him, I would draw and shoot him and whoever is behind him in the hallway. Next it would be the Pastor. After that, out the doorway, and see if Tammy would pull the trigger. If she does ... I grin, and the Pastor who is in my face trying to calm me steps back.

I know that look. I take a deep breath and mentally step back from what beckons me. It is a reluctant step back. I say, "It's okay. I'm good." The Pastor does not look convinced.

I feel what I had touched slip away. Now I just feel tired. I just want to go. Anywhere. I also know I have to say the right thing now. Even better, I know what to say.

"Really. I'm okay now."

I pause, and then follow up with, "Pastor. That was one hell of a prayer. You got the Spirit working in you. Yep, you sure do." I am nodding my head like an idiot.

He looks at me, thinks about it, and decides he likes that a lot. He smiles hugely. "Why, son, the Spirit does come upon me. Yes, it does." I feel the arms holding me relax, and then let go completely at the Pastor's nod. I look around. The guy holding me actually has hair and a pretty good tan.

He is big too. He stares back evenly. Zeke is standing in the hallway and looks like he is having problems processing what just happened. Looking at the one with the hair I know I was right in deciding to shoot him first.

I push past Zeke who is looking at me like I am some kind of freak. *Fuck him.* Tammy is standing at end of the hallway, no shotgun in hand. "It would have been a clean getaway," goes through my head. Behind me I hear the Pastor telling the other two, "Did you see that! That was the Spirit moving in him. Damn! I knew he was different..." I block out the rest of his bullshit as I approach Tammy who steps aside for me uncertainly. I tell her, "It's cool. I'm blessed. Not distressed," and smile. Her eyes dart down the hall and back to my face.

"The Pastor says you have an address for me? A job doing security?"

"Uh...sure." I follow her back to her desk and watch as she pulls a folder out, looks inside, and then writes on a piece of paper and hands it to me. I look at it.

2900 Heather Anne Lane. Annandale. See Brother Bob.

She even added a little smiley face with a halo at the bottom.

"Very nice," I tell her. "Thanks."

She smiles, looks down, and then up at me through her eyelashes. It probably was devastating when she was younger and at the front end of burning her life down.

I hit the door trying not to look like I am in a hurry. Once I am outside I stretch my legs and make the first turn I can to get out of the line of sight. I have no desire to give these assholes my fingerprints or social. I hear my name called but I just keep going.

Now the Asian stores are starting to fade. They seem to be hanging in there but food prices are going up and you never know what is going to be scarce. There is probably more to it than that but my curiosity doesn't run that deep. The only places that seem to be expanding are the Middle Eastern ones. I guess being at war there for over a decade was good for business. On the surface it doesn't make sense but I've noticed most of the ethnics we have running around are from some country we've bombed the crap out of and then occupied. When I realize that, I spend some time daydreaming about what life would be like around here if we attacked Scandinavia.

Walking into the kiosk erases any dreams of Scandinavian honeys as an Indian Grandma displaying too much belly greets me. I pause for a second before I continue in. I formed this habit after striding into a convenience store back when I had a job and catching the end of a robbery. They were on their way out and I ended up holding the door for them. They wore masks back then, and were in a hurry, neither of which is needed now. One of them muttered "Thanks" as he went past. Good manners are not easily forgotten.

Today, I don't get any sense of trouble. An Indian couple is bitching at the clerk about rice. I catch something about Basmati and how hard it is to find now. Apparently US rice sucks and is too expensive. They are speaking English. There must be a lot of dialects in India because they almost always seem to use English when they do business with each other.

Although the kiosk started out as a store, most of it is empty now. What food they have is behind the counter. The DVDs for rent or sale take up more space than the food items. The floor racks are mostly gone except for a couple of shelves for dollar store stuff that no longer sells for a dollar. The rest of the space is used for computers: four computers, all three years old at least. That is fine with me. You don't need a quad processor to surf the net and read email. Two of the four are in use. One by an employee, probably the owner's kid; the other by an older guy who is a dreamer. I say that because he is on Monster.com. The only computer jobs hiring, that I know of around here require a Top Secret clearance. That is hard to get when your address is "fluid" and you only know your character references by AKAs. Not that I have the niche skills they are looking for anyway.

Junior gets up from his computer looking annoyed, and asks what I need.

"Computer time."

"Three US New an hour."

I count it off and give it to him. He looks at it, and points to the machine next to the dreamer. "Time starts now." He walks away and I settle in. Damn, it feels good to be back on a computer. My laptop has been down for a week because the crappy fan Acer used in it died. It is the only item, other than my iPod, that I had taken into the wilderness. The iPod I had sold.

I cannot part with the laptop, even with it being broken. It is stupid I know, but a part of me feels like as long as I own it I am more than just another homeless guy. At times, I fear the very real possibility that I might fall through the cracks and end up as just another bum sitting on a milk crate getting waffle ass. Sometimes, though, I welcome the idea. It would be so easy to just give up and see where it all leads. What stops me is I know what giving up means. It means becoming vulnerable. It means becoming prey. No way am I ever going to let that happen.

I check my email. I am not sure why I bother. It isn't like anyone is trying to keep in touch. I check the Spam folder out of habit. Much to my surprise I have an email from Night. It is short, simple, and makes me feel surprisingly good.

"Be Careful. Come Back."

No problem there, I think. I start running through my

usual news blogs. In Yemen the Marine Expeditionary Force has taken casualties, and given twice as many, while chasing evil terrorist bands of some sort. Saudi Arabia looks like it is having real problems with civil unrest. Gold is headed for 2k an ounce. I read a side story about graves being dug up by scavengers looking for gold teeth.

I decide to get serious. Mapquest gives me the location of the address. I check the street and aerial views. The aerial view doesn't tell me anything, but it makes me feel like a Special Forces guy doing an insertion or something cooler than checking into a freaking Jesus lovers' homeless shelter where my new job is to protect them from something. Probably more like protect the staff from the "guests" and cold cock obnoxious drunks.

I tell myself I will do it only until payday and then head back to the Anchorage. The email from Night was interesting. Maybe if things work out I can get free rent. I type out a short reply for her to pass on to Max. I let him know where I have been and where I am going.
Then I get daring. I add "*Miss you*" to the end.

I log off and head out the door. The walk to the house is just that - a walk. I spend almost all of it agonizing over whether I should have added those last two words to Night's email.

Chapter Thirteen

Brother Bob's house is a brick-faced colonial in a neighborhood where every other house is a brick-faced colonial. Bob himself answers the door. He is maybe 50, balding, 5' 10" and 170 pounds.

"You Gardener?" He looks and sounds really tired.

"Yep."

He sticks out his hand and we shake. As we do, he steps forward, leans into me, and sniffs. He isn't all that subtleabout it either. I know he isn't checking to see if I need a shower. I shrug it off. It is probably the standard routine with him. He looks me up and down. He doesn't say anything about the Ruger but he doesn't miss it either.

I follow him down the hallway past a faded "Palin - Beck! Stop the Wreck!" poster. Over his shoulder he tells me I can call him "Chief." He explains that he was in the Navy. That's nice but I don't see the connection. Not that it really matters; he could tell me to call him "Bunny Lips" as far I am concerned and I would.

He leads me down the hallway to the kitchen and tells me to take a seat while he makes us some coffee. I like him a lot more already. He unlocks one of the cabinets and pulls out the can of coffee telling me, "We're all good Christians here but why tempt anyone," and then he shrugs.

Indeed. I look over his shoulder and see that Bob has done all right by himself with the goodies. He even has chocolate chip cookies in there but, much to my disappointment, he doesn't offer me any.

While he busies himself with the coffee, I look around the kitchen. It looks like any other kitchen except for the two posters hanging on the wall. One is a large picture of

Jesus - the blond version, of course. The other lists the "House Rules." Bob sees me looking at it and says, "You might as well memorize them." They are pretty simple.

1. Behave. Jesus is watching. I read that and remind myself to look for web cams.

**2. Weapons will be checked in and out with staff.
No drugs or alcohol use will be tolerated. This includes cigarettes!**

3. Church and Bible study attendance is mandatory.

4. No guests!

At the bottom it says, "**Remember! When in doubt, ask Jesus!**" Somebody penciled in "or the Chief." That this has not been erased tells me a lot. Then again, as far as I know, Chief may have written it on there himself.

He hands me a mug and says, "The milk is in the refrigerator but check the expiration date." He sits down. After I check the milk's date, sniff-check it, and pour some into my coffee, I put on my listening attentively face.

"This is how it is. Everyone here right now is squared away. You need to be here to check them out in the morning and check them in when we open again in the afternoon. Nobody stays inside unless they are sick or working the night shift. We don't have much of either."

He goes on for a bit and catches my attention again when he says, "They will be calling you over to the other house soon enough. You guys never stay here long before you move on." He says this with an air of resignation. He also says it like I have a clue what he is talking about. I don't, but I am not going to tell him that.

Then he shows me around the place. It doesn't take long. I have my own room. That is nice. It even has a padlock on the door. I actually have four keys to carry around now:

two for the locks on the front door, one for my padlock, and one for the armory which is in the hall closet. Chief tells me, with a shit-eating grin, that the cost of the padlock will be taken out of my first check, along with the automatic 10% tithe, taxes, and other fees.

"So what's my take home, Chief?"

I am stunned when he tells me, "Oh, probably about a third of what you thought."

He sees my face. "Yeah, they never tell you new guys that. Hey! Think of it this way. You're working." He walks away laughing.

The thing is, being able to say "I got a job" does make a difference. In the house, out of twelve guys - the standard number for these places, only three of us work, and I am one of them. The other two are Bob and a guy named Chris who works for Dominion Power as a lineman.

Chris keeps to himself. He is the object of envy and resentment for some of the guys, which is probably why he stays aloof. Also because he is likely tired of people hitting him up for a couple bucks. It doesn't take long for me to get tired of that either.

Some people think that if you have a job it is your duty to hand a few bucks out to them on demand. One of the guys even goes as far as telling me, "Jesus would want you to give me a dollar." I just stare at him, and then I say, "I'm hearing Jesus right now and he is telling me to break your jaw." He opens his mouth and gets as far as "But that's..." then shuts it and leaves me alone. It's a good thing that he does because I wasn't kidding.

The next couple of weeks go by fairly fast. I spot a webcam in the kitchen and don't bother looking for more. I enjoy the bible study, much to my amazement. The Jesus in the book turns out to be a lot more interesting than the one on the wall in the kitchen.

Also there are the Cougars for Christ. That's what I call them. They are ladies who come by to help us understand the Word. They like me and I like them. After the second class I start going out with them afterward for coffee. We sit around and talk. It is all about caring, sharing, and Jesus. Then Lynn gives me a ride back to the house. She may be getting up there in years, but she has enough contortionist in her to make the drop offs last for an hour or more.

Then one day the routine changes. I am downstairs, sitting in the kitchen, and staring at the lock on Chief's cabinet. "Cookies and coffee!" my brain is screaming. "Just pop the lock!" My brain does not understand webcams, right from wrong, and the need for stealth.

I have already checked everyone out for the day and am free for a couple of hours, at least in theory. The reality is I usually end up doing yard work or painting something. I don't mind. Sometimes Chief sits and watches me, and tells me stories of his misspent youth aboard various US Navy vessels. Chief had been a serious drunk in a Navy that no longer tolerates it. How he got by as long as he did before finding Jesus and retirement is a mystery to me.

Today, as usual, he comes down dressed for work. In his case, that means khaki pants and a khaki short-sleeved shirt with black dress shoes. At first I thought he put a hell of a shine on them until I realized they were plastic. The first words out of his mouth are, "You squared away, Gardener?"

"Yeah, Chief. I'm all sharp edges and sunshine."

I never know how to respond to that so every time he asks, I make up shit. I am pretty much stuck on the "Sharp edges" reply at this point.

"Good. They want you at the 'House' in an hour. I'll run you over."

He unlocks the cabinet and makes us some coffee. That part goes unsaid too. I wait every morning for him to come down to make us coffee. I still haven't been offered any cookies but I figure it is just a matter of time.

"So what's up with that?" I ask him.

My mission to find the people that had burned the Chinese is starting to fade. I kind of like it here. Lynn is going to have me over for dinner in a couple days and I am looking forward to us having a large flat surface to play on. I had casually mentioned her to Chief. He looked at me, chuckled, and told me to buy some vitamins. I think he might be on to something there. Chief is an easy boss and life is good. I have gotten a little slack on doing my fast draw reps in the morning but I am still good.

"I don't know. They never tell me and I don't ask. They told me to tell you that you need to bring all your stuff."

"I'm not coming back?"

"Nope. You guys never do."

He goes over to the cabinet, grabs the cookies and sets them on the table. "Go ahead. I've seen you eyeballing them." I eat six cookies in the blink of an eye. Chief watches me and is amused. "You like cookies?" I nod my head, as my mouth is rather full. "Go ahead and take the bag. I'll see you downstairs in thirty minutes."

I am downstairs thirty minutes later. My Transformer bag now holds two pairs of underwear, socks, three t-shirts, and another pair of pants. That is my first week's pay. Everything except the socks and underwear were previously owned. I also have a paperback Bible that Lynn gave me. Chief had mentioned that I should buy a shirt with a collar for church services. He didn't volunteer to pay for it so I didn't bother.

We get in the "Chief Mobile." It is a Buick Lacrosse that is only a few years old. Chief must have only drunk the cheap stuff because he seems to do all right by himself. I guess spending half his life at sea made it easy to save money.

As we head down Route 236 I ask, "You know anything about this place?"
"No." He hesitates then tells me, "Well, yeah. Scuttlebutt has it that the church has some plans to build 'Base Communities.' I'm not sure what that is about. It sounds like urban compounds or neighborhoods."

"So what's that got to do with me?"

"Maybe the people that already live there don't want to move."

He changes the subject. I try getting back to it, but he won't go there after that. I know he has more to tell, but I also know that he isn't going to be the one telling me any more.

We drive into a gated subdivision. Chief waves a magstrip and the gate opens. I notice an SUV parked where it can watch the gate. I can't see in because of the tint but I know someone is in there watching us. We don't have far to drive, just a few blocks. There aren't a lot of houses in this development. He pulls up in front of a cul-de-sac that is fenced off at the entrance. Chief doesn't have a card for this gate. I gather up my bag, tell him thanks, and swing open the door. I am about halfway out when he calls after me.

"You get jammed up. Come on by the House."

"Yep."

I get out of the car and head for the gate. They have an actual guard booth like the ones the rent-a-cops have in front of the government building downtown. It has a pedestrian entrance built into the fence next to the car gate. I have to give my name and wait while the guard checks on me with someone. After five minutes he opens the gate, points at the house on my left, and tells me to go check in.

Chapter Fourteen

I am not the only one who has been told to show up here. I am the last one to check in. That means I get to walk into a room full of posturing men and two women who are semi-amused but loving it. The one standing by the fireplace is obviously butch but that isn't slowing the males down any. The other is the classic American field hockey girl. There is a feeding frenzy around her. I go and sit down in a corner to watch and wait.

I'm not the only one who has made that decision. A handful of guys are already sitting in the corner; ones who know they don't have a chance of making it through the outer ring surrounding the women, or don't want to bother trying. I look them over. Compared to the guys flocking around Field Hockey Girl, they are right. Pasty white, short, overweight, geeky. Pick any tag, and there is a guy sitting there, just like I am, that it fits.

The woman who checked me in told me I am in the "B" group. Looking around I have a pretty good idea of who else is in the B group. The guys with hard-ons for the women look like vets. Based on some of their tattoos, the weapons they are wearing, and the t-shirts, they probably are.

My crew, well, let's just say if I had a choice I wouldn't want to stand with them against the A team. One of them, standing next to Field Hockey Girl, is obviously the big dog. At first glance most people would look past him, instead focusing on one of the weightlifters. I don't. He might as well have a flashing sign over his head that says "Kill Him First!"

He isn't as pumped as the others. He is more quiet. He isn't the tallest either. He doesn't even have a cool death dealing graphic or unit t-shirt. He is wearing a plain white one; the only one of them that is. But even Butch is giving him the eye. The rest of them give him a little more space, and I notice they listen to everything he says when he decides to say something. Mostly he just stands there, smiles or laughs, and scans the room constantly.

I must be violating the two-second gawk rule. I have a bad habit of doing that. Carol is the one who taught me that rule one afternoon when we were spending our lunch period getting high. We had finished, and were just sitting there watching the parking lot from where we sat on the side of a hill. She broke the silence, asking, "Did anyone tell you about the two second rule?"

I, of course, had no clue what she meant. Hell, I had been wracking my brain for something to say to her as it was. I think it was one of two times I actually had been alone with her. "Ah...no" was my reply.

"The two-second gawk rule means you never stare at anyone for more than two seconds or they will know you are staring at them."

"Oh."

Then I realized that I had been staring at her. I usually did whenever I had a chance. Now though I felt like an idiot. I wanted to tell her I gawked because I thought she was the most beautiful woman in the world. That just sitting here watching the breeze touch her hair was the best thing that ever happened to me. Did I? No, of course not. We sat there silently for about ten minutes. Then she thanked me for the buzz and left. I spent about an hour on the side of that hill hating myself after that for not telling her, or least talking to her.

I remembered the rule though and tried to practice it from then on. I must be violating the rule now because White T-shirt detaches himself from the crowd and heads towards me.

He stops in front of me and quietly says, "I'd like to take a look at your weapon if you wouldn't mind."
I am very particular about anyone putting their hands on my Ruger. Yeah, I am aware of the sexual connotations but for me it is more a matter of vibes. I believe anyone that handles my personal gear leaves a part of themselves in it. It is about as close as I come to a religious belief. With this guy though, I stand up and slip it from the holster and hand it to him. Of course the room doesn't go silent but everyone watches while pretending not to. He looks at it, flips open the gate and closes it, then balances it in his hand.

"Nice weapon. Hard to find a Ruger like this nowadays."

He says it loud enough that everyone hears. He goes on about the .357 as a killer round and Rugers in general until everyone's attention drifts back to Field Hockey Girl. As he hands it back to me, he says, "Max knows." Then he turns around and walks back to the group.

I sit back down and think about that. What does he know? I don't know anything other than I wish I could have stayed at the House. Now it looks like I am going to miss my big date with Lynn. She even has cable for her TV and high speed Internet. I am in love. Instead, here I am, sitting with the B squad. I'm not really happy about that. I barely look up when I hear "All right people. Listen up!" This comes from a new guy who just stepped into the room. *Shit*, I think, *I'm stuck in a B movie with the B squad.* This strikes me as kind of funny and I laugh out loud. Unfortunately it breaks the silence that follows our being told to "Listen Up!" That does not go over well. I sit up straighter and shrug an apology to whoever the hell he is.

He looks like a Disney movie gym coach, but he has a better withering glare. I know because he is practicing it on me. He then introduces the man who is standing next to him. I recognize the name. This is one of the guys Max wanted me to find. I am not impressed. I never liked spray tans, especially on white guys who look like Central Casting's

idea of a successful executive or Baptist preacher.
I just know he is a golfer, has a blond second wife, and
drives a sporty car. I want to shoot his ass right then and
there. That would probably not be a good idea though. So I
stay sitting up and listen to what he has to say.

He is full of shit. That much is obvious fairly quickly.
But it is warm and sincere shit that appeals to the people I
am sitting with. It is 40W oil slick shit. It goes something
like this:

"We are in strange times -- I believe it is the End Times.
You are special. Why? Because you have been chosen
twice: once by God, and then by me. You will be warriors
for God and our people. Are we racist? No! A thousand
times No! We just wish to preserve our culture -- our
language -- our identity!"

I notice everyone is raptly listening and nodding
along with him so I start nodding too. Especially as Coach,
who is standing next to him, is checking each one of us out.
He goes on for another fifteen minutes and then finishes
up.

"We are family. What happens in the family -- stays in
the family. You will be taken care of. You will not be given
burdens to carry that are too heavy. I do know you will
make God, your country, and us proud!"

He gets a standing ovation, which he eats up like it is
fresh cookies from the oven. Then he says a short prayer,
blesses us, and leaves. He doesn't take Coach with him
unfortunately.

Coach gives him a few beats to clear the door and
then announces, "All right. A Team, to your quarters. B
Team, sit tight." Yep. I was right about who belonged to
which team. We sit there and watch the vets go. They leave
without making a big deal of it.
Well, most of them do. A few look over at us and grin. A

few say, "Later." Field Hockey girl is the only one smirking as she passes us. Butch, to my surprise, winks at me. I wink back. Coach catches it. I am beginning to think he is one those guys who has built in radar for catching people like me. I sit there thinking, *Stuck with the support staff and copier clowns again.* The reality is I don't have the vets' credentials. It is the truth. I know it, and it is bitter.

Coach looks us over, and tells us, "No. You are not them. That doesn't mean anything. Somebody saw potential in you or you wouldn't be here. If it makes you feel any better we are putting together a training camp just for people like you." That perks most of the group up. The military is no longer an option for guys like these. They aren't hiring. They are firing. It costs a lot of money to occupy faraway places and the USA just doesn't have it anymore. He likes the idea that we, well, most of us, can't wait to go to bible boot camp or whatever the hell they call it. Myself, I already decided that when the day comes for us to leave for it, that will be the day I am gone.

"Well, men, I suppose you want to know what you're here for." He pauses. It is only for dramatic effect, because he doesn't wait long enough for us to ask. "You are going to be part of a pilot program. We call it 'Sanctuary' because that is what we are going to build." The short version, as best as I can tell, is we are going to be census takers for Jesus. The church has decided to colonize a neighborhood with true believers. The plan, at least what Coach sees fit to reveal to us, is simple. We will go to this neighborhood, starting tomorrow, and find out what houses are empty. If they are not empty, then we will record who lives there, including their ethnicity and religion, which I think is interesting. When he mentions that part, he laughs and tells us, "Don't worry, most of them are Spics who shouldn't be here." He laughs again. "I mean Latinos." We all laugh along with him. Well, almost all of us. I don't, and I notice one of the other guys doesn't either.

There is some more of that. Then he says a prayer and

tells us we will be bunking in the basement of the house next to the A team. He cuts us loose and we head for the door. I am not surprised when he calls my name. He waits until the rest have left, then he asks, "You okay with the program?" He is doing the caring father figure/counselor/sharing routine. It is bullshit. I look at him. I mean, I look at him hard, and say, "When the shit goes down, I'll be there." He doesn't know how to take that, but it sounds close enough to what he is fishing for that he swallows it.

"Good. Good."

He puts his arm around me and walks me to the door. "That's what we need. Fire and steel."

He likes that so much he says it again. "Yep. Fire and steel."

He pauses and looks at me; "You know you can talk to me anytime." I tell him, "Sure," shrug off his arm, and hit the door. I realized something in our walk to the door. Coach likes his "Boys." I decide I will kill him if I get the chance regardless of how this all turns out.

Chapter Fifteen

Our new quarters are not as nice as what I had back at the House with Chief. I don't see any sign of potential Cougars for Christ either. I am going to have to figure out a way to get word to Lynn once someone tells me what my schedule is going to be. There has to be some free time available and she is 'churched.' They will like that, I hope.

Our quarters are downstairs in the basement. Senior staff has the upstairs. There are nine of us. We have cots and no privacy. Our group leader, Eric, is from the neo-Nazi church, and gets the only bedroom in the basement. He tries to come off as a combat vet, but it turns out he had been in the Coast Guard and did his time on Lake Erie. He got out early with a medical due to an E. coli infection he picked up from the water.

"His war wasn't hell. It was shit," is how Luther, one of the guys in my team, describes it.

We are divided up into groups of three. Mine includes Abe and Luther. Luther constantly surprises me over the next few days. He is honestly devout. He even spends time in prayer when he doesn't have to. I was prepared to hate him, but find him to be a decent and funny guy. Abe is the youngest of us at nineteen. He is easy going and a totally committed believer. Both of them are from military families; each has parents who are high up in the church and have active duty commands.

Generally I like all the "trolls" - our name for ourselves -that live in the basement. Yet, at times I am amazed at how casually stupid and racist they are.

I am also amazed at how they take for granted that they are somehow superior and entitled to a standard of living that is, it appears to me, only sustainable by living off the work of others. The same *others* they hate.

I get really tired of hearing the word "blessed." I come out of the bathroom one morning and casually announce that I feel blessed that my bowel movement had been of superior quality. Do they bat an eye? Hell no. Instead one says, "The Lord is good."

The next morning, after a good breakfast by my standards, and some half assed instruction, we are all loaded into a van and dropped off at the subdivision we are going to census. Each three-man unit from the B Team is assigned a section of it. We are given a clipboard, which has a printout of the addresses, a map, and a form to record what we find out.

We look sketchy to say the least. No white shirts and ties for us. We get nametags sealed in laminated plastic attached to our shirts with safety pins. My safety pin breaks immediately. Below the name, in English and Spanish, it says that we are "Social Outreach Workers" and has a little smeared seal printed below it. It looks vaguely official. I don't see what will motivate any sane person to open their door to us. Since I am getting paid, I really don't care all that much.

The van drops us off and we stand there watching it as it pulls away. Luther shakes his head, half mumbling, "I feel like a Mormon." Abe, who I am to find out is Mr. Literal, tells him, "We aren't Mormons. We're Christians."

"Yeah. We don't have ties, bikes, or a clue." I tell them. I think it's funny. They don't.

"We do too have a clue!"

Abe holds up the clipboard that he has been put in charge of. "See?" I just shake my head and look around.

I know this place, not well, but I have been through it a few times over the years. It is right off Route 7 and is one of the oldest planned developments around here; at least sixty years old. It is officially named "Pimmit Hills" but I know it as "Primitive Hills." Supposedly it had been an all white, blue collar, druggie, and biker-infested dump for most of those years. That was before my time.

The Primitive Hills I know is a mix of white, Middle Eastern, and Spanish people. The real estate crash had been brutal here. I know that from a coworker who had lived here and had his house foreclosed. He tried to sell it but told me, "It's hard to sell when half the houses on your block are either 'For Sale' or owned by the bank." These are little box houses built a long time ago, not McMansions. By the turn of the century most of them would fit inside the great room of the average new house being built around here.

The prices for them had gone to the moon anyways. They were conveniently close to a regional mall, and DC Metro Transit was going to push a subway stop to it. They had almost finished building it before they ran out of money. Supposedly the Feds are going to take over and finish it, but I don't see that happening anytime soon. The US government is broke. It didn't help when the market crashed and people found out the fifty-year-old 1000 square foot house in Primitive Hills they had paid $400k for was dropping in value every day. They walked away in droves. Those that didn't walk hung on until they were pushed out for not paying the mortgage, usually after living rent-free for a couple of years.

This doesn't mean everyone is gone. It is a huge development, and people still live here. Just not enough people to keep the neighborhood from slowly falling apart We stand around while Abe shows us our map. Luther gets us oriented, and then says, in amazement, "This place is big!" It is. I already knew that. They are just learning it. We have at least a couple weeks of work ahead of us.

We were dropped on the eastern edge of Pimmit Hills, which stops at Route 7. Based on our map we are to start on the first street to our right and work our way up. I brought my Transformer bag with all my worldly possessions in it minus the bible. It is too heavy and I know finding another one will not be a problem. I also brought a bottle of water that I filled from the bathroom tap and a roll from breakfast. My two team members brought nothing. I know I am going to have to start checking taps at the empty houses for water. These two are going to be complaining of thirst within an hour. I just know it.

I am carrying everything I own because I am not sure if I am going to stick around. I have some of the information that is my reason for being here. Based on White T-shirt's comment Max knows what I know. Hell, he probably knows more. Lynn the Cougar will probably be available whether I am here or not. I don't think she comes with the job, although that would be an interesting perk. Tough to advertise though. So why bother sticking around?

I mull that over as we approach the first house. Money? That is always a problem. Returning with some would be nice. This job pays far better than working at the House did. Night is not going to let me sleep at the Anchorage for free. Well, she might, but her parents, or whoever the hell they are, would probably frown on it. I am still thinking it over when we stop in front of the first house. Abe checks the address against our list and says, "Yep. This is it." Then he reaches to open the gate. The house is fenced with four foot high chain link fencing that surrounds the entire front yard.

I grab him by the arm just before he opens it.

"Hold on, Abe."

He looks at me, looks at my hand, then back at me. I see, just for a brief second, another Abe. I don't much care for him either. *Fuck him*, I think and let go. As I do, a pit bull comes around the corner moving like a shark that has just smelled blood. He hits the gate hard, bounces off, and starts telling us what he would like to do to us if he gets the chance. "All right, everyone. Let's step back. I think we need to talk about how we're going to approach houses here," I tell them. Abe's hand drops to the 9mm he is wearing. "Don't, Abe, unless you want to start a war. Come on, y'all. Let's go sit under that tree."

I see movement inside the house through the window. Just a shadow crossing but I don't like the feeling I am getting. I can tell Abe doesn't want to go. The dog scared the crap out of him and he wants to make it pay. Luckily Luther touches his other arm, telling him, "C'mon, brother. Let's go sit down. We can come back." I look across at Luther. His eyes cut to the same window. So, he had seen it too. Abe hadn't. He can't take his eyes off the damn dog.

"Let's go."

I turn around and walk away feeling an itching between my shoulder blades as I do. The other two follow about a step behind me.

We sit down underneath an oak tree in an overgrown yard across the street. I realize as we walk across the street that I am going to stay; at least until we finish the job. Much to my surprise I feel I owe it to Luther and Abe. And I can use the money. They, despite all their talk, really have no clue what the world is like out here. I also like Luther. He is the first Jesus lover I have known who I think actually has something going on. He is a genuinely good person much to my surprise.

I pull out my water bottle and pass it around. After taking a swig, Luther asks, "What tipped you off about the dog?"

"The piles of dog shit. They weren't little either."

That got both of them nodding their heads.

"Look, this is how I think we should do this. All of us don't need to go up to the door. We are going to scare the hell out of people. If it is a fenced yard, we check it first. Look for a dog house."

"Or large piles of dog shit," Abe says and laughs.

"Yep. If it has a sign saying 'No Trespassing' we skip it. For the others, one of us stays on the street while the other two go to the door. When we get to the door, only one talks. The other hangs back about four feet or so. We don't want to make them feel threatened. What do you think?" They like it. We have to work out the rotation and who is going to get to go to the first door. Abe gets that, which makes him happy. It also makes me happy. I have the sidewalk. Abe can catch the first round, and I can cover Luther's withdrawal. We mark the house with the dog as *"Occupied. Race Unknown. Mean Dog in Yard."*

Then we check the house whose yard we are sitting in. It doesn't feel occupied and it isn't. Luther waves me in from where I am standing after peering through the front window. I walk up to the house. Both he and Abe are peering in the window now.

"Gardener," Luther whispers, "take a look. The place is trashed!"

I look in the window quickly and don't see anything I haven't seen before. I realize these two have never been in a foreclosure before, or if they have, it wasn't a downscale one like this.

"Luther," I tell him, "nobody is home. You don't have to whisper."

Abe thinks that is pretty funny.

"You guys want to go inside?" They do.

"Is the front door unlocked, Abe?"

"I don't know. I didn't try it."

It is unlocked. They look at me. I look at them.

"Oh well."

I draw the Ruger, step inside and yell, "Hello! Anybody home?" Then I quickly move from there to the middle of the room and listen. Nothing. I know the place is empty but I hope they are paying attention to what I just did. My sense for an empty house has never betrayed me but why take chances? The one time it does will probably end up being a painful, if not fatal, mistake.

They draw their weapons too. It is painful to watch. Luther has some fluidity but Abe is a fumbler. They are bad enough that I tell them, "It's cool. Put them away." I have no desire to get shot in the back by accident.

They look around, stunned. The odor of urine doesn't help. It isn't bad by my standards. I have scavenged in worse. The original owners left the sofa. Someone had taken a knife to the cushions and tossed chunks of the rubbery yellow stuffing around the room. There are empty beer cans and rubbers on the floor. Nobody bothers collecting the cans anymore because no one is buying them. I notice Abe staring at one extra large condom on the floor by his feet. I ask him, "What's a matter, Abe? Never seen a midget's condom before?" He just shakes his head instead of answering. Hopefully he has never seen one before and I have just given him a complex about the size of his dick.

I check the kitchen and quickly back out. I have never liked flies, and I have no desire to find out what is in the sink attracting them. Abe has to look. All I hear is an "Ewwww." They want to see all the rooms. The bedrooms have more trash, clothes, and a stuffed animal. Abe kicks at a paper he finds on the floor. It says, *Nuevas Raices,* which looks like Spanish to me. I guess it does to Abe too. He kicks at it again and mutters, "Damn Spics. Shit all over everything. Come to our country and ..."

"Shut up, Abe."

This from Luther? I am impressed. I am glad he said it, because if he hadn't -- I would have. Abe looks offended and surprised but he shuts up. They look around one more time. I am starting to think of these guys as my foreclosure tourists. Then we, well, Abe, writes it up, and we move on. The rest of the day is more of the same.

I ask Luther if he is okay when we both have door knocking duty. He looks surprised, then smiles and says, "Yeah, I'm good." I leave it at that.

Chapter Sixteen

Over the next few days we settle into a routine. They find themselves some water bottles and we are given sack lunches to eat when we are dropped off. Luther turns out to be good at talking to people. Abe gets arrogant with them whenever he thinks he can get away with it - usually with old people and foreigners, which is just about everyone who answers the door.

I am surprised at who talks to us, who they think we are, and who blows us off. The Middle Easterners, and there are more of them than I expect, think we are from the government and bog us down with their complaints and requests for assistance. The Afghanis are the nicest. They give us tea and little bread snacks. I like them. The Iraqis just complain and think we are going to pull out our wallets and pass out debit cards.

The other ethnicities are polite, but when they find out we are not giving out anything, they shut the door. Luther and Abe are amazed at how many different countries the people come from, especially since, as Abe puts it, "They all look alike." Supposedly these two have lived all over, but I am beginning to wonder if "all over" really means different towns in Iowa or North Dakota.

The Latinos are shy, polite and just want us to go away. The Whites? They are all over the place. Some want to shoot us I think, but because we are white and polite, they hold off. Instead they offer us beer. Some are Christians, and once Abe and Luther hit them with some code words, they invite us in. I even get cookies a couple of times! They also are a great source of information about the neighborhood. I recognize some of the gang tags I see but I'm not sure if they are real or just wannabees. The Whites tell us about the gangs but I am not sure if they mean *Gangs* or if they have just seen groups of guys with brown skin hanging out, and hung the gang label on them.

The gang question is answered when we are cruised. We hear them before we see them. Luther and Abe just stare as they roll by. Luther says "What the..." The car is a Honda Civic. No surprise there. The wing on the back is wide enough that four large pizzas could be stacked side by side across it. The windows are tinted but the job was not professionally done. It looks like black Saran wrap was glued over them and they didn't quite get all the wrinkles out. Primer is the primary exterior color. No expense has been spared on the car's sound system. I call them heartbeat cars because the bass resounds in my chest cavity like the heartbeat of a giant. They roll us a couple more times that day but that is it. The street stays quiet the entire time and no one will answer their doors.

The neighborhood is starting to change. Not so much the physical look as the vibrations it is putting out. I noticed that earlier without really registering it. Now it is becoming obvious. On a single block the composition of families and their ethnicity changes from one end to the other. Sometimes I am sure I can actually smell it changing.

One thing never changes for me. When people open their front door to us, it is like being granted a look into another world, from the pictures on the wall to the wall they hang them on. The walls are always painted in a different color from the previous block's color scheme. The smells drifting out and the music coming from a radio or iPod player somewhere inside change. Even the physical appearance and attitudes of the people who open the door changes on each block.

I have experienced this before in houses I scrounged though or slept in. Those, though, had been empty shells. Only the bright colors of the walls remained. That and the trash with different brand names or languages than what I was used to. On really slow days I would sit and look at each piece of trash and try to figure out what it said. Sometimes I would find CD cases, usually empty inside.

The cover designs and people on them fascinated me, especially Indian ones. I am sure the women on those are from a different planet.

Abe is beginning to irritate me and, I think, Luther too. He manages to find a way to do it differently for each one of us. Abe is a multi-faceted kind of asshole. For me, it is his habit of closing one nostril and blowing a load of snot out the other. Spring means allergies for him, and this year there is no allergy medicine to be found, or so he claims. We will be talking, and he'll stop, casually turn his head and blow a load out, then pick up where he left off. That is if he doesn't get a hang fire, which requires finger intervention.

For Luther I can only guess why Abe grates on him. He is not one to speak ill of others. My guess, based on reading his expression, is a dislike for Abe's hate-fueled spewing about the people we come across. That doesn't bother me as much. I had a couple of "Uncles" that talked the same kind of shit.

I am starting to wonder if some Latino kid had given Abe one too many wedgies in third grade and scarred him for life. He bothers me because he is a clueless dumbass who needs constant watching to make sure he doesn't get us into something by his inability to read situations.

So far the job has been relatively easy and interesting. After getting cruised by the gangbangers, I have a feeling that may change. Being raised the way I was, and then being homeless, means I always have, for lack of better words, a Threat Evaluation Program running. It runs continuously in the background of my consciousness, evaluating the world around me. It focuses primarily on people as they are usually the source of the most pain. It was running my survival odds against the gang boys with a backup consisting of Abe and Luther. It doesn't like the odds and is telling me in no uncertain terms that it is time to go.

Abe, besides being keeper of the clipboard, is also the keeper of the phone. We were given, well, Abe was, a cheap Virgin Mobile phone to use in case of emergencies.

Instead of calling 911 we were told to call the programmed number, report our location and the nature of our problem. My guess is the response will involve dispatching the A Team.

The next day we get cruised again. This time it is a little slower and the guy riding shotgun casually shows us his handgun. It isn't very big but Abe is impressed. He yells, and I mean yells, "Holy Cow! Check that out!" I see it and so does Luther, but we aren't broadcasting to the entire neighborhood that we are dumbass rookies. Luther tells him to shut up before I can.

If I had the phone I would make the call right then. Not for a pickup; rather I would ask for a drive by of our own. Just to let everyone know that we are not out here alone. Now I have to decide whether to ask Abe for the phone. Either that, or convince them to end the day early. I know that, either way, I am going to sound like a pussy. My mind says, *"Just walk away and don't look back."* The other half answers, *"Don't be an idiot. Tomorrow is payday."* Then, out of nowhere, I hear a new voice. It says, *"Fuck it. Let them come."* I laugh inwardly. I like that answer the best, but payday wins and I ask Abe for the phone.

"The phone? Why do you need the phone?"

He genuinely doesn't get it. "You sick?"

"No. I'm not sick. I think we need to request an A Team drive by."

"You got to be kidding. Hey Luther! I think he's scared."

He laughs, and looks at Luther for support He doesn't get any. Luther tells him, "He's right, Abe. Let him have the phone, or you call it in."

Abe stares at him, and then shakes his head in disbelief.

"You're both pussies."

He digs around in his bag, finds the phone, and hands it to me.

"Here. You call them. I'm not taking the blame when they bitch at us for wasting their time with this chickenshit."

I take the phone. I remember him showing it to us and telling us about the programmed number during a break on the first day. I hit it, and put it up to my ear. It rings twice. A voice says, "State your emergency." I so want to say something like "We have Heathens inside the wire. I repeat, 'We have Heathens inside the wire.'" Instead I say, "We could use a drive by. You know, let people know we aren't out here alone." I know it sounds lame as soon as I say it. For an answer I hear "Please hold." I look at the guys and roll my eyes. About a minute later the voice says, "Please confirm your location." I tell them where we are. They pause for about ten seconds, then I am told "Arrival in two minutes" followed by a dial tone.

"We got company on the way. Two minutes."

Abe looks scornful.

Luther sounds calm. "Good."

Two minutes later a fast-moving blue Chevy SUV rolls up. Two guys get out. Both are big, wearing armor, and have black military-looking rifles hung around their necks on slings that keep them in front. They look like shrunk down M-16s. I have seen them before online but I can't remember what they are called.

Both are wearing sunglasses. When the driver gets out, he stands by the vehicle and begins looking around. The other one asks me, "What have you got?" I give him a brief rundown of what we have seen and been told by the neighbors. He stares at me, scratches himself under his armor by his hip, and says, "Yeah. When they start doing the drive by shit you know it's a just a matter of time before something shakes loose. We already had a problem west of here this morning."

That is news to us.

"What kind of problem?" I ask.

"Oh, some ragheads and one of your teams didn't

hit it off. Words were said. It got out of hand. Some noses were broken. Nothing serious." Abe's eyes widen. He asks, "Any shots fired?" It sounds to me like he really hopes so. "No. No martyrs today," he replies grinning. He looks around, then back at me. "You want us to make a couple passes, let our shit hang out? Then park for a bit?"

"Yeah. Sounds good," I tell him.
We talk a bit more and then they mount up. They roll down the street playing Toby Keith's old song "American Soldier" at max volume. We watch them go and then go back to our work. Our effort is mostly wasted because nobody will answer their doors for us. We end up marking half the street as *"Empty"* or *"No Answer. Possible People."* They pass us once more as we head back to the pickup place. The guy in the passenger seat holds his weapon out the window and shakes it as they go by.

We finish up and wait to be picked up. I don't like that we are just standing here. It feels far too exposed but I can't see a viable alternative without hiding outright. I know that will not go over well, and the idea of doing it grates on me. Instead I just stand there, waiting, and nodding in the right places to Abe's stream of bullshit.

I look at the houses that comprise the leading edge of Pimmit Hills and know something has changed. Something that is going to severely cramp, if not cut off, my supply of cookies. I see smoke coming up thick and gray from what has to be a burning house not far from where we had been earlier.

We get in the van when it comes, escorted by the same blue SUV that showed up for us. Inside the van everyone is buzzing about how the other guys got their asses kicked. One of them had drawn his weapon, then had it taken away by one of the displaced Iraqis they had been talking to. It had gone downhill from there. From what I hear the Iraqis taught them a lesson in how to properly conduct themselves in other people's homes. I am probably the only one who sees it that way though.

One of the guys sitting in front of Luther and me turns around in his seat and asks us quietly, "Any of the people you talk to mention the rumor that's going around now?" We both look at each other and shake our heads though I swear Luther, from his expression, knows more than he claims not to. Even more quietly, enough so that we have to lean forward, he tells us, "It's a land grab." *No shit*, I think. "*So that's the plan*, I thought. I ask him "You mean like carve out a White Christian enclave." He continues, shaking his head, "No, it's not like they said. They are going to force these people out by making them sell for nothing to a Church front company."

"Yeah. And your point is?"

I don't get it. Why is he upset about that? I look at Luther who in turn looks at me like I am the idiot here. He tells the guy, "I know. I have been seeking guidance." The other guy thinks that makes complete sense. I am lost here.

"Huh? What?" I ask Luther.

"Later," is his only reply.

Chapter Seventeen

Later is slow in coming. We are too closely packed and, I am sure, monitored, for it to happen inside the house. Instead Coach gives us a "Buck up, stay the course, and don't take any shit" speech after dinner. It is well received by my fellow campers from the basement. Then we pray, and share our concerns until it is time for lights out. I figure out later that is what it was supposed to do.

The next morning I eat a quick breakfast and go outside to practice my reps. It has been a while and it shows. Not a lot, but I can feel the difference. Only the last few feel right. Then it is off to board the van. The driver hands me my bag lunch and I drop it in my Transformer bag. A lot of the guys bitch about the quality, but nobody returns them. I think they are quite good. I am going to miss the daily baloney sandwiches and vending machine crackers.

We get dropped off at our regular place. The feeling of uneasiness hanging in the air has not dissipated. If anything, it has increased. I feel it. I know Luther does too. Abe is oblivious and raring to go. The first time Abe asks us, "What's a matter?" he laughs after asking, and it is obvious he thinks we are scared. The second time, after lunch, he genuinely wants to know. "The shit is getting ready to hit the fan." This I know without a doubt. Of course after I tell him this he begins looking around for gunmen to pop out of the shrubbery. There aren't any of course. Nor is anyone outside again. When Luther and I pair up for door-knocking duty I ask him, "What's up?" He tells me in snatches as we go from house to house. "The Church wants to own this development and they got a lot of money riding on the successful outcome."

"Who the hell wants to buy a development full of old house? Plus this place is huge." Even I know that is stupid. "Yeah, except they don't have to own every house at first. Think of it as a chessboard. They only have to control the center. They are using the same tactics we used in villages and towns overseas. Control certain areas, own a critical mass of people, and you own the place. Of course you may have to disappear, or encourage to leave, certain groups ..."

We pick up the conversation where we left off at the next house.

"Okay, Luther. I understand that, I think. But where is the benefit? The money. Who makes money on this?" He grins at me. "It's all win for them. Especially if you know ahead of time what areas are going to be included in the new Security Zones." He lets me mull that over. I have one more question and one more house to ask it. "Luther, how do you know this?" He looks away, and then back at me. "It's hard to explain. You ever read the *Ender* series? You know, *Ender's Game*?"

"Yeah."

"Well, I'm a graduate."

Then he looks at me, laughs at my expression, winks, and tells me, "That's top secret by the way."

We continue on. Sometimes, ahead of us, I see kids outside playing but they disappear as we draw closer. No one answers doors. Music goes silent. Not even the white people answer. One woman stares at us through the front window but makes no move to answer the door we have just knocked on. Only the occasional dog barks at us. Nor is there a drive by. It is quiet. Very quiet. At least until late afternoon. Then we start hearing gunshots off in the distance. "Gunshots," Abe states. I guess he isn't sure if we can tell the difference between them and the birds chirping.

"No shit," I reply.

"Should we call in?" Yeah, looks like Abe is getting

nervous. "No," both Luther and I answer. I let him finish, curious to hear his reason why. "We got two more houses. Let's do them and head back." I agree. Abe also does, reluctantly. My reason for finishing up is a bit different. I am hoping they will come. Damn, I am actually praying they will. My prayer is answered.

And come they do. Driving down the center of the road, bass thumping, radiating hostility. We are walking down the sidewalk heading to the next house when we hear them. We have been walking single file. It is the easiest way to navigate what is called a sidewalk, but better resembles the teeth of someone from West Virginia. A lot of missing, twisted, and cracked concrete slabs with some green poking up here and there.

We tighten up instinctively. Abe is in my back pocket all of a sudden. I step out into the road and watch them roll in on us. Luther steps away from me and onto the road to my right. Abe doesn't move. They stop about fifteen feet down from Luther, idling the engine as they sit there. The tint is too dark for me to see more than faint shadows inside the Honda. The music goes silent and the doors open. I start walking at an angle towards them. I want them closer and I also want a better angle on the guys getting out on my right. Since I am left-handed I would prefer to switch places with Luther but such is life. I almost reach the spot I want to be at when it begins. In theory I suppose I should be worried, but I am not. If anything the same calmness I felt back at the shelter is easing through my body like a hit of good dope, or a shot of whiskey on an empty stomach. I like it.

The Leader is riding shotgun. He shuts the door and stands there smiling at us. The passenger door opens and another guy steps out to cover the Leader's back, so the two guys on my side are out now. The driver is also out, on Luther's side.

My guess is we are all working from the same script. Leader will say something. Luther or I will respond. Leader will say something derogatory and laugh. His crew will join in. Then he will draw his weapon and make some kind of demand of us. Probably one that will humiliate us. They are bad asses, but I don't think they are LA-style bad asses. Hell, they had probably been laying tile, cutting lawns, and cutting carpet a couple years ago. Regardless, I am going to kill them.

As soon as Leader opens his mouth I shoot him in it. Then I shoot the other guy on my side. I drop to a crouch, run up to the car and shoot the driver who is just standing there gawking at me.

As far as I can tell I am the only one who has drawn a weapon. Leader has one tucked into his waistband as does Gawker. I look inside the car and see a shotgun on the floor where Leader's feet had been a minute or so ago. I wonder why he hadn't come out with it. Well, he isn't going to be telling me now.

I look at Luther who is just standing there looking all bug-eyed, and sigh. I guess his battle school or whatever the hell he was talking about didn't have this on the curriculum.

Abe is busy throwing up. I tell him, "When you get done barfing you might want to make a call." I repeat it to make sure he hears me. Then I tell Luther, "Time to take a walk. Come on, Abe. You can puke as you walk." Then I start walking slowly. I don't want to leave them. I just want to get them moving. It works.

Abe catches up to me first. Jesus, his breath stinks. He hands me the phone and won't meet my eyes. I barely hear him mumble, "You make the call." My ears are ringing. I shake my head. That doesn't clear it. Oh well. I take the phone, thumb the preset, and listen to the ring. I have no idea what to say. After a couple rings I hear the same message, but in a different voice this time: "Hello, state the nature of your emergency."

"Hi. We have three dead bodies and a really ugly car available for pickup."

There is a pause. I can't help myself; I grin.

Then I hear "Say again." I repeat it. "Please hold." That is what I expect. I don't expect to get patched through to the Pastor himself. "That you, Gardener?" I can hear a voice whispering in the background.

"Yep."

"Tell me your situation, son."

His voice is calm, reassuring, and radiates concern. I briefly outline what happened. When I come to the end he doesn't hesitate with a response. If he had I would have bailed right then and there.

"No problem. You sure your boys are all right?"

I tell him again that they are. "Then you just stay there, stay calm. Help is on the way."

I hang up and slip the phone into my pocket. Abe is the first one to ask. I knew he would be.

"What did he say?" He is almost able to keep the fear out of his voice. I look at him. I look at Luther. I look back at him and wait a few beats. Then I tell him, "We'll be in his prayers." I enjoy Abe's bleating blast of "What!" Even Luther looks rocked for a second. "Just kidding. Help is on the way, my brothers." Then I grin. Luther shakes his head, tries to grin back, and tells me,

"You are really an asshole."

"Yep," I reply. "That I am."

We stand there waiting. Fortunately we haven't walked very far; maybe fifteen feet. I notice Luther and Abe keep the bodies behind them. Out of sight, out of mind. The street stays quiet. No one comes out of their houses. Over to the West someone rips off a short burst of automatic gunfire. It doesn't help Abe relax.

I am going to give the Pastor two more minutes to show up with something. If he doesn't, then I am gone. Even Fairfax County, whose response times have dropped from under five minutes to twenty-five plus, would roll on three dead people. They might even put the chopper up in the air. I think they still have one. Which reminds me of something. Why have we not seen a single patrol car since we have been here?

I am mulling that over when Abe tells me - he doesn't ask - he tells me; "You executed those people." I look at him. "When did they quit being Spics and become people, Abe?" He doesn't have an answer. "Because they were always men to me." I stare at him until he looks away. Luther, much to my annoyance, won't let it go. "Why did you shoot them down like that?"

"Are you fucking kidding me?"

Only the fact that he looks genuinely puzzled stops me from going off on him. I take a deep breath and look at them both.

"You two really think I executed them?"

I can't believe it when they both nod their heads.

"Jesus H. Christ. What did you think was going to happen back there? What exactly did you think we were going to do? Have a fucking prayer meeting? You think they were coming by to discuss the situation?"

Damn, I am getting angry.

"Huh? You two fucking lame ass wannabe militant supremacists for Jesus are asking me! You limp-dicked sonofabitches who never drew your fucking weapons? At a minimum they were going to kick our asses. I don't know about you two but I am not going to sit around and wait for an ass-kicking."

They are backing away from me now.

"Someone comes at you with hostile intentions and guns in their waistbands and you're going to fucking debate?" I am yelling now.

"Oh, I know. You want to wait until they make the first move? Is that it?"

Fucking Abe nods his head. Instead of exploding I just look at them. Despite all the talk, despite wearing weapons, and despite the fact they could have died just minutes ago, they don't have a clue. I find I am no longer angry with them. It is like a switch has flipped inside me.

I look at them and shake my head. "God help you." I

walk away to await the Pastor's arrival.

Chapter Eighteen

The first arrival is the A Team. White T-shirt is running them this time. They have a black SUV just like the big boys downtown. He also has it lit up with the red and blue lights they use. I start walking towards the vehicle.

White T-Shirt watches me approach, scans the block, and talks to his people at the same time. I can feel Abe and Luther fall in behind me. I don't look back.

His people look professional - professional in the sense that they are fully geared up including helmets and microphones. They look like CNN images of US troops from any one of the crappy, hot places the troops have been sent to in the last few decades. His guys fan out, forming a perimeter around the vehicle and the bodies.

"Hey, Gardener."

"Hey." I never got his name.

"You two get in the vehicle and stay put." Luther and Abe, without protest, climb in and shut the door. White TShirt shakes his head, walks over to them and opens the door. "Leave the doors open, guys." He comes back to me and asks, "You okay?"

"I'm fine. How about you?" Why the hell is everyone asking me if I'm okay?

"I'm Scott." He sticks out his hand. We shake and he adds, "Walk me through what happened."

We walk over to the bodies. I am getting bored with this. I notice the flies responded the fastest. They have already landed and are doing whatever the hell it is that flies do.

I tell him, "I stood there and shot them." He nods his

head. "Yeah. You sure did. Nice shooting. You use that Ruger?"

"Yep."

"Damn fine weapon. Okay guys...toss them in the back. Glenn, park the Honda and leave the keys in the ignition." He holds his hand up to me, says "Yes, sir" into his mike, and turns and walks away to continue the conversation in private. His end, from what I can hear, entails repeating "Yes, sir" four or five times. When he is done he walks back to me and says, "You're riding with us. Hop in with your team." The back of the SUV settles as the last body is tossed in. He tells his people, "Two of you get to ride in back with the meat. Let's roll."

I get in back with Abe and Luther. I was hoping Abe would have managed to wiggle his way into a window seat. Instead he is in the middle and still reeking of vomit. The "meat" is already starting to spoil and the flies are making the journey too. Nobody has to be told to roll down the windows. It is a quiet ride at first. The only conversation is from one of the guys in the back.

"Goddamn it. His fucking head is leaking on me."

Everyone, except Abe and Luther, find that funny. After about ten minutes of driving, I say, "Hey, Scott. What happened to the Pastor?"

"He canceled."

He doesn't bother to look back at me when he says it. "Probably someone advised him it might not be in his best interest to be seen in the same place. You never know who has a camcorder."

"Shit." I hadn't thought of that. He must be watching my face in the mirror. "Don't sweat it. Everything is wired."

I think about that the rest of the way, which turns out to be to a shopping center where we stop in the empty parking lot. Empty except for another SUV. This time it is a teal colored one. SUVs are cheap now. It is the gas that is expensive, really expensive. Even priced in new dollars someone is spending serious money on this.

"All right, guys. Time for you to catch your ride."

"Scott ..." I slide forward a little bit and ease the Ruger halfway out. "What's up?"

This time he turns around to look at me. I know he sees my hand resting lightly on it, my thumb on the hammer.

"We aren't going near the house with fresh meat in the back. You get to ride back with them and we get to go find us a backhoe." That makes sense to me. The guy who complained about the leaking head adds, "Thank you, Lord."

We get out. I get out on Scott's side. As I walk towards the waiting SUV Scott calls to me, "Nice shooting. You're good. But you wouldn't have gotten out of my vehicle alive if I didn't want you to." I look at him. "Yeah. I think you might be right." He starts to grin until I add, "But you wouldn't have walked away either." I grin back at him. He tells the driver to roll and they pull away. I watch him watching me in the mirror until they make the turn onto the main road.

The ride back is uneventful. We go right into the compound. When we get out Coach meets us and takes us to the main house. Here we walk through what happened again with him. It doesn't take long. I am brief, and the other two, well, they don't have much to say.

He sends the other two on their way and tells me to have a seat in the waiting area, which was once the great room. It is nice. They have comfortable chairs and a sofa made of real leather. Very nice.

What makes it perfect is the flat screen television, over the fireplace, tuned to Fox News. They are doing a segment on the European riots. Spain is a mess. A bankrupt government and an official unemployment rate of 27% are the cause, at least according to Fox. The same is happening in England. Scotland is reportedly getting ready to announce their withdrawal from the United Kingdom. They also mention the Baltic and Finland, which are in total chaos.

No video from there. Probably too small to waste money on sending a camera crew and Fox is probably too cheap to buy footage from the locals. I want to see if I made the local news but they have hidden the control and I am to lazy to get up to manually change the station.

After a 45-minute wait I am ushered in to see the Pastor. He gets up, comes around his desk, shakes my hand, and has Coach get me a Coke. We say a prayer praising my work today in the name of Jesus and then he gets down to what he wants to say. He starts off by asking me if I am okay. I tell him I am. Then he praises my actions again and tells me how they need more young men like me. I am a credit to my family, my country, and my God. I agree with him.

Then he pauses, and stares at me. Afterwards I realize it was his famous piercing stare. I get up, thinking it is time to go. Plus he is creeping me out. Startled, he waves me back down and gives up on the stare.

"Gardener, I know you don't see the big picture here. In time perhaps you will. We had our doubts about you."

He chuckles, as does Coach who is sitting in on this. Then he continues. "But no federal agent would have done what you did today." I nod my head while thinking, *What the fuck?*

"So we have decided to move you up. You and your team are going to be in the first class of students at our training academy."

He beams at me, waiting for my overjoyed response. "Well, gee...that is really great." Then I smile. Rather my face twitches. I was never good at fake smiles but it passes muster with him.

"Good!"

He slaps his desk with the palm of hand to emphasize how darn good it is. "I want you to hang around here the next few days. Let's see how the wind blows." He stands up again and leans over the desk, his hand outstretched. We shake, he gives me his blessing, and

Coach shows me the door. Coach doesn't put his arm around me this time. Good thing. I might have smashed his artificially whitened smile to smithereens with the barrel of the Ruger.

I don't know what they have planned. After all I don't see the big picture. I do know that fifteen minutes after I walk out of his office almost every SUV in the compound pulls out of there in a hurry.

I find out later that one of the census teams was ambushed as Pastor was finishing up his quality time with me. They were walking down the street and were hit by a drive by. All of them went down. The other census teams were quickly called and told to get in a defensive position until someone could come by to extract them. They burned the midnight oil until early in the morning at the big house after that.

I spend the next day lounging around. It is nice. I go swimming. One of the compound houses, the one the A Team uses, has a pool. It is probably unofficially off limits to lower echelon people like me but I don't care. Besides I am getting tired of this. Two more days will make it payday and then I'm gone. Hell if I am going to bible boot camp.

Chapter Nineteen

Then things change like they have a habit of doing.
After dinner we are assembled for a meeting. Coach lets us
know that there is a new plan and we are all going to play a
part in it. We are going back to Pimmit Hills tomorrow and
we are going to kick some ass. Or as he puts it, "Break the
back of the Satanic Resistance!"

The others applaud with varying degrees of
enthusiasm. I just sit there and look at him. I've always hated
pep rallies. When the applause dies down I ask, "What
Satanic Resistance would that be?" He looks at me like I just
farted in church.

"Why, those that shot our brothers down in cold
blood."

"They're satanic? You know for sure they are his
Infernal Majesty's minions?"

"Yes. Of course."

I just stare at him. Then I ask him quietly, "Did you just
call me an idiot?"

"No. Of course not." He is starting to look a little
uncomfortable.

"It sounded like that," I tell him.

"No. No. I mean..." He is definitely looking
uncomfortable now. I like that.

So I say, "Okay. You want to give us a little more
detail? Like are these minions easily recognizable? Is there a
plan? What is our role?"

He takes a deep breath. I am scaring the shit out of
him and he doesn't know how to deal with it.

"We are going to hit a few houses that are known centers of neighborhood resistance. The goal is to scare them and render their homes uninhabitable, thereby demonstrating that it is in their best interest to relocate." I think he is surprised by what he just said. I know I am, and out of the corner of my eye, I think a few others are too.

"So we're going to burn them out?" I ask.

"Yes. Well ..."

"Thanks, Coach," I tell him.

I want to ask, "Is there is going to be a BBQ afterward?" Or maybe, "Are white sheets optional?" Instead I stand up and walk out. As I pass Coach I pat him on the shoulder. He flinches.

In the basement that night it feels like I am now in a bubble. The rest of the guys are polite but they are also reserved. I don't feel shunned as much as I feel excluded. I don't understand why and it bothers me. I have spent enough of my life feeling like an alien that it is an all-too-familiar feeling. Not one I like either. I would like to talk to Luther but he is kneeling by his cot praying. I don't want to disturb him. Hell, maybe God really listens to his prayers. Instead I go outside.

It is a beautiful night. I'm not sure but it seems like this year I can see more stars at night than I ever have before. I look around. There is nowhere to go really so I go back to the pool. I think I'll sit in one of the lounge chairs and watch the pool. Maybe slip in and swim a little bit to burn off this unease I feel. That is if it is empty. I don't feel like dealing with anyone.

I slip through the gate and stand there. The water looks beautiful lit up from the lights in the pool. To me pools are magical. I never know why. Maybe because the few good times I can remember as a kid included them. We would stay at a motel and if we were in the money it would have a pool. Mom would take me to it every day. She was always happy about it. I didn't realize then that to her a pool was just a place to fish for fresh "Uncles." She always found one, and I ended up with a lot of pool time in the afternoon.

I am just settling into the lounge chair when the sliding door that leads from the house to the pool slides open. I watch the silhouette move towards the pool. For a second I think I might get lucky and it will be Field Hockey girl. Maybe she will even want to swim nude in the moonlight. Instead it is Scott. I see the flash of his grin and return his greeting. He settles into the chair next to me, lights up a cigarette, sits back and smokes. We don't say anything. He just sits there and together we watch the pool glow in the dark.

I am getting ready to get up when he says, "That wasn't the first time for you was it?" I know what he means.

"No."

"I thought so."

He grinds the cigarette out on the ground and starts to tear the butt into strips of filter fiber. "Your people over there acting weird about it?"

"Yeah." Now he's got me curious.

"Giving you more space?"

"Yeah."

He sighs. "Everyone will. Well, almost everyone. It's the way it works."

"The way 'what' works?"

He looks over at me, and then goes back to watching the water. I don't think he is going to answer but I'm not going to ask again. After a few minutes he says, "They know now what they probably have already sensed." He pauses. "We're wolves and they are sheep. We kill sheep. They don't like that but, being sheep, there isn't a whole lot they can do about it."

I think about that. I don't like it.

"What if I want to be a shepherd?"

He sits up. "Well, it fits with the general Jesus thing they have going on here. The problem is there are a hell of a lot more wolves these days."

"Yeah. Well, I think Max is a shepherd."

"Shit, Gardener. Max is a fucking werewolf." He laughs.

"Tomorrow you will see for yourself. A lot of people will. That's why I'm out of here."

He gets up. As he walks away he says, "I'll see that nobody bothers you. Unless Cathy Lynn isn't busy."

I don't say anything. I wait for an hour. No one comes out. I didn't think they would. Still I wait for another hour just in case. Then I go back to the basement.

Everyone is asleep. One of the guys in the other team is trying to jerk off quietly. He was obviously not expecting anyone. I grin as I go past him. At least he isn't breaking wind like someone else is. I am seriously tempted to grab my blanket and go sleep outside on the deck. Instead I undress, roll into the cot and am gone in seconds.

We get paid early the next day instead of in the evening. I am surprised; my envelope includes a bonus. We are paid in cash: US new dollars minus our "expenses" and automatic 10% tithe. The tithe is in lieu of Social Security I figure. I never expect to see anything from either one of them.

My bonus is half of a gold coin. It looks and feels good in the palm of my hand. I want to bite it like I have seen and read about but I have no clue why people do that. Does gold have a special taste? I make sure no one is looking and put it in my wallet.

They send an A Team guy - not Scott - into the basement where we all have to gather. He inspects our weapons; well, everyone's but mine. I refuse to let him touch mine. He lets it slide. Then we have to practice drawing and the proper stance. A little late I think. I leave and go to watch television but the cable is down again. I end up sitting on the deck reading an old Steven King paperback that I found in the great room. It's okay. I've read it before but I like vampire stories.

It isn't hard to feel the nervous energy in the air. It continues to build as the day progresses and it is starting irritate me. Much to my surprise Luther comes upstairs and sits down across from me. I am at a good part in the book so I only look up, greet him, and go back to reading. He sits there silently for about fifteen minutes, and then I guess he realizes I am not going to look up again so he says, "Hey, Gardener."

"Yeah?" I turn the page without looking up.

"You feel bad?"

I sigh in my head. Well, maybe physically too.

He holds up a hand. "Look, if you don't want to talk about it, well, I understand." I am not dense. I know what he wants. This is the cue for serious "Caring and Sharing," the bonding shit I have read about and never understood.

"Luther, it's like this. It's no big deal."

Then I go back to reading. About ten pages later he gets up and leaves. I keep reading.

Twice more people disturb my reading, both times to ask if I have seen Scott. Nope is my reply each time. Scott is gone. He never shows up. Word is he disappeared sometime in the night.

Chapter Twenty

I am thinking about taking a nap when Abe summons me. "Time to mount up, Gardener." I go downstairs, grab my Transformer bag, and stuff the Steven King novel into it. Then I go outside and get my seat for the parade. That's what it feels like. We pull out as part of a convoy of SUVs. In the lead is a Porsche Cayenne. I ask the driver as I get in, "Who's riding in the Porsche?" He looks at me like I am an idiot. "The Pastor." In this case he's right. I am an idiot. Who else indeed?

We are briefed on the way by one of the A Team people, the same one who ran the firearm inspection. Two SUVs per house. Two houses per SUV. We are going to hit the first one at dinnertime. Our job is to provide outside security while the A Team people go in and kick everyone out. Then we are going to burn the house down.

"That's kind of harsh, isn't it?"

"You not with the program, Gardener?" he asks me.

"Oh yeah. I'm good to go, hot to trot, and ready to take it to the next level."

He doesn't know how to take that. Nobody does actually. I just grin at him. He has shades on so I can't read his eyes. I hate that. If I were king, no one would be allowed to wear sunglasses when they were around me.

"Okay. I'm good with that," he replies.

I nod like I actually give a shit.

We hit Route 7 and roll west towards Pimmit Hills. Traffic is light and the conversation almost nonexistent. Almost nonexistent because every so often Abe tries to say something witty or "We're going to kick ass." It is met with silence. He looks down at his hands. A mile or two passes;

he tries again and gets the same results. I find it rather entertaining.

We follow the Porsche and the SUV with the A Team assigned to us right on Pimmit Drive passing our usual drop-off point. The other two SUVs continue on. They are going in on Paxton Drive, which is further west on Route 7. I am not surprised the Pastor stays with us. In fact I would have been surprised if he did not. Our vehicle holds most of the rookies who, with the exception of myself, have come from good families. Their tithes probably paid for all the SUVs I have seen. He has to be seen during this, and he has to be seen by the rookies most of all. Plus, and this doesn't occur to me until later, he has to make sure nothing happens to them.

Once we make the turn into Pimmit Hills I feel the tension in the people around me ratchet up a notch, especially when we turn onto the street where our first target is. As we roll past one house, one I know is empty, I notice an Asian guy is sitting in the driveway in a folding chair reading a paper. At his feet is a long neck Budweiser. He may be the first Bud-drinking Asian I have seen in my life. I am still going through a mental list of Asians I have known and if I have ever seen them drink beer, let alone a Bud, when we pull up in front of the house.

We have arrived, swooping down like overweight birds of prey in our SUVs. The first problem is parking. I guess they assumed there would be plenty of curb space. There isn't. There had been a couple days ago, but now there are a handful of cars parked along the street, and in front of the house. The Pastor ends up double-parked while the A Team's vehicles find curb space a little farther down then they originally planned. Our driver wedges us into a parking place but his double-parking skills are a little rusty and we end up bumping the cars in front and in back of us. By the time he gets us parked and we exit the vehicle, the A Team people are forming up.

The next problem rears its chain link head.

The yard is fenced. There is a gate for the driveway and another gate from the sidewalk leading to the front door. The A Team planned to go in through the driveway gate but it is locked with a combination padlock. While they work that out a couple of pit bulls arrive and are waiting for them.

The rest of us stand there on the sidewalk in a clump in front of the gate leading to the main door. I listen as the vaunted A Team people yell things like:

"There's a dog!"

"Who has the bolt cutters?"

"What! They're with the other team?"

"Damnit! Shut them dogs up!"

This is not going well. The driver of our vehicle returns and places a 5-gallon gas can on the sidewalk. *Very subtle*, I think. Meanwhile people are coming out of the occupied houses and staring.

Luther is standing next me and nudges me, saying, "Oh no." Faces appear in the windows of the house that is our target. Hispanic faces, including an older woman with gray hair. He is right. We have an "oh no" unfolding, especially when I see the kids' faces. They are smiling and making faces at us and at each other. I see the older one - he is about eight - push his sister, cousin, whatever, who is maybe five out of the way so he can see better. He flips us off.

Coach gets out of the Porsche and tries to take charge. I look back and catch a glimpse of the Pastor's face. He has his window down and is watching the show. I watch as he gets out and stands there, looking undecided.

Coach yells, "Shoot them dogs!" Someone does with a quick burst of gunfire.

The A Team regroups and picks up their battering ram or whatever they call it. It is probably called a "Tactical Door Opening Device" or something equally stupid.

The front door of the house opens and a middle-aged Hispanic male comes out yelling, "What the hell are you doing?" A couple of neighbors from the house two doors down begin walking up the sidewalk towards us. They are young men and I mark them as targets.

Luther mutters, "I am not doing this. I am not." He turns around and gets back in the van. Meanwhile I keep watching the kids watching us. "If Max is coming, he'd better get here soon," goes through my mind, because there is no way in hell I am going to let this get much further along.

Chapter Twenty-One

Everything begins happening at once. Later I think of it as being like a pool table that is awaiting the first shot. The stick is drawn back, and then it snaps forward, just like the hammer of my Ruger being cocked and then released. Once the cue ball smacks into the freshly racked balls, there is brightly colored chaos spinning across the felt playing surface. Abe is the one who makes the shot that releases ours.

The Hispanic man standing in the yard yelling at us quits yelling when he sees his dogs get shot and his gate get unlocked by a large man kicking it off its hinges. He begins backpedaling towards the front door yelling, "Marta! Call 911!" Marta, probably his wife and mother of the kids, comes out the front door screaming something incomprehensible and brandishing a large kitchen knife. He starts marching back down the sidewalk towards us, with her right behind him.

The two neighborhood guys coming up the sidewalk flinch when the dogs are shot, then crouch and begin reaching under their shirts. The entry team sees this and reacts by dropping the battering ram and moving towards them. The rookies are watching all this take place like they are at home in their media rooms. All except Abe.

He casually walks through the now open front gate, past the entry team, draws his 9mm, and shoots the Hispanic man high in the chest near the left shoulder. Hispanic man begins reaching up, trying to touch it. Marta really begins shrieking.

I draw. I am a touch too slow to stop Abe from getting off the second shot. He misses, but if I had been practicing more he never would have gotten it off. I don't miss. I hit a little forward of his ear and take most of his jaw off. One of the census takers behind me is screaming.

I am gambling that none of them are going to join Abe in shooting anyone but I still have the driver behind me. I pivot, cock and shoot him in the throat. He had begun drawing, most likely to shoot me in the back, and had moved a fraction from where I expected him to be.

I bolt through the open gate, run up the sidewalk, and push Hispanic Man and Marta towards the front door, yelling, "*Niños! Niños!*" That gets them moving, especially when we all see the little boy who flipped me off watching us wide-eyed from the door. Marta screams, "Juan!" and takes off for him, her husband stumbling after her. I follow them, moving backward so I can keep an eye on everyone.

The A Team people have finished with the two neighborhood guys. They are down, and the sidewalk has far too much blood on it for them to still be alive. They are shifting their attention, and weapons, back to the front door, which means me. Not a good thing. The only thing that gives me that extra second I need is it still hasn't clicked that I am now foe rather than friend. I accelerate backwards using my height and weight to push Hispanic Man through the doorway.

That works except I hit him too hard. He stumbles, probably from the combination of being pushed and the pain from being shot, and falls as we go through the door. I am watching the team and I go down as my feet get tangled up in him. I had been getting ready to shoot the one next to the man with the battering ram as he seems to have the most wits about him. He does and I watch as the muzzle of his gun points at me. My shot goes wild as I go down and his round goes through the space I just vacated and takes a chunk out of the doorframe.

I fall backwards on top of Hispanic Man and hear him grunt in pain. Too bad he isn't a typical American. It would have made for a far more cushioned landing for me. Instead he is all wiry muscle and bone. I scramble off of him and crouch. I yell, "Marta! Niños bathroom!" I know there has to be a bathroom on this floor. Hopefully they still have the original iron tub. The Hispanic man yells something at her too. I hear him muttering behind me, "What the fuck is these assholes' problem?"

Instead of answering, I hook the front door with my foot and try to shut it. It only shuts about two thirds of the way. At least we can't be seen from the street now. Marta comes back with a dishtowel and is fussing over her man, trying to get to the bullet wound so she can look at it. He pushes her away, takes the dishtowel, presses it against the wound, and tells her, "Not now, Marta. Take care of the kids."

I tell him, "We got to get out of here!" I am looking around the living room. On top of the curio cabinet is a folded American flag in a case. Next to it is a picture of a young Latino man in an Army dress uniform. About one second after I focus on it wondering if it is what I think it is, a burst of fire blows out the window, the TV, and the flag with its photo to pieces.

"Sonofabitch," I mutter. I help Hispanic Man up and backpedal towards the kitchen. I want to be back far enough that I can watch the front and the back of the house. Thank God these houses aren't that big. Another burst hits the side of the house, punching its way through a couple of walls on its way past us. I lay flat and take him down with me doing it.

I look over my shoulder. Marta is on her knees looking out the open door of the bathroom. We back up enough that I can see in. She has two of the kids in the bathtub and the other is curled around the toilet. They look at me, all big brown eyes and scared faces. Damn! The rage shoots up inside me like a flash fire. I check out Hispanic Man. He looks fair to middling as far as functioning. I slide him the Ruger. "Cock it to shoot. Don't let them get the kids. Understand?"

He nods. Marta is watching from less than two feet away.

Chapter Twenty-Two

"Give me the knife!" I hold out my hand. I take it; the knife has an eight inch stainless steel blade with a black plastic handle, probably dishwasher safe. It is getting hard to talk. I don't want to talk anymore. I want to move. Hispanic Man is saying something. I ignore him. He is just background noise now. I sprint forward, low and fast like I am coming out of the blocks, and go through the gaping hole that had been the front window.

I am lucky the glass had been blown inward instead of outward or I would have eaten some of it for sure. That would have hurt later. Instead I lose my balance as my momentum drives me forward but manage to make a three point landing on my knees with my right hand open, slapping the ground and keeping me upright.

One of the memories that I will always retain from that day is the dandelion next to my hand and how yellow it is. I don't believe I'll ever see another as yellow again.

I look up. Life has changed out here considerably in the few minutes I have been gone. Others have arrived and a gun battle is taking place in front of me. It is hard to see who it is. The SUVs in front of me block my ability to see who is on the other side of them.

In front of me one of the census takers is on his back. A couple others are crouching next to the SUV and look scared witless. The rest have moved to join the entry team and are taking cover behind their SUV. The entry team is firing at whoever is on the other side of the Great Wall of GM that divides us from them, using their vehicle and the

Pastor's for cover. It doesn't look like it is working out too well for them. The best part is the Pastor. He is crouched by the rear of the SUV we came in. He has his cell phone out and is busy texting -probably a prayer request that the "Big Guy" send him some help ASAP. Well, his prayers have been answered. Just not the way he expects.

From my right I hear one of the entry team yell, "Out!" Nobody is focusing on me, except for the two scared census takers and I don't think I am really *there* for them. That is fine with me. I am not interested in them either as long as they stay put. Instead, I zero in on the Pastor. I sprint towards him. There is only one way I can see to do this and it is going to hurt me more than him at first. I hit the chain link fence running, grab the top gray steel support with my right hand, swinging my body up, and letting my momentum carry me over the top.

I go through the air sideways and slam into the side of the SUV. That not only hurts, it stuns me for a second. I have my eyes shut on impact but instead of stars I see shooting rays of gold and red against a background of black. I slide down the side of the SUV just like in the cartoons.

I am back on my feet in seconds. I tucked the knife against my body as I went over the fence. I still have it, but I must not have held it right, as the blade cut a gash through my shirt. It is bleeding and so is my nose. I wipe the blood from my face with the back of my hand and stare at the Pastor. He stares back at me in total amazement. Later I will remember his expression and laugh. Now I move. He is trying to talk to me, to stand up in reaction to me coming towards him while he continues to text.

Behind me someone comes over the top of the SUV, clearing the fence, and hits the ground without stumbling and begins firing on what is left of the entry team in short bursts. I have no clue who it is, especially as I am just beginning to see movement and shape with my peripheral vision. I really hit the side of that SUV hard.

I don't stop moving. I hit the Pastor and take him down with me on top. I don't clutch the blade to me this time. I bury it in him. I am screaming. My face is close enough to his that I could lick him. He is screaming, "Stop! Stop!" My arm is pumping like a piston, driving the blade in, back out, in him, and back out. He stops screaming, looks at me puzzled, and asks, "Why?"

I can't answer him. I am somewhere else and seeing faces I have not seen in years.

I hear a voice telling me, "Gardener ... Gardener. It's okay. You can stop."

I recognize the voice. It is Max. At the same time I realize that the world is quiet except for someone sobbing not far from me. That is annoying.

I look up at Max's face. He reaches out, touches me on the arm, and tells me, "Come on. Get up. We don't have much time."

I stand up and look around. The house looks like something you would see in an old Terminator movie. It is pockmarked with bullet holes and no windows are left in place. The front door is still ajar.

Behind me only one of the census takers is still alive. That is where the sobbing is coming from. There is no sign of Luther. From the number of bullet holes in the SUV it is highly unlikely I am going to be seeing his head pop up. The entry team is scattered in the positions where they had fallen on the ground. One is draped over the hood of the SUV they had taken shelter behind.

I look over to see Scott talking on a cell phone. He nods to me, says "Done deal" into his phone and clicks it shut. He tells Max, "One minute to drive by."

"Drag them out."

He looks at me. "Keep the knife. We need to toss it later. Where's your weapon?"

"Inside."

"Get it. We are moving in two."

I head into the house, stopping at the door to yell,

"Marta!" before I go inside. I hear kids crying and see Hispanic Man watching me warily from the hallway. It is more than a little strange looking down the barrel of my own gun.

I tell him, "It's over. Point that thing somewhere else." He sighs, says, "Marta," softly, and sets my gun down.

"Thank you," I tell him.

Marta pops her head out and Hispanic Man says, "It's over," softly. She bursts into tears and hugs him.

Out of the corner of my eye I see a black Mercedes S Class sedan roll slowly down the street towards us. Max has just finished dragging the Pastor out from behind the SUV. Scott has done the same with Coach. The rear window of the Mercedes rolls down and I see an Asian face look out, see the bodies, and nod. The Mercedes accelerates down the street. Max has fulfilled his contract.

I stick my head in the bathroom. All the kids look okay but scared to death. I smile at them. They respond by looking more scared. *Oh well*, I think. I tell Hispanic Man,

"I'll take my gun back."

He places it in my open hand and says, "Thank you. We owe you."

This is true but it also is wrong. I dig into my back pocket, pull out my wallet, and give him my piece of gold. "For the kids," I tell him. Then I walk away.

The End

The Lion

by nova

Flying Turtles of Doom Press
Copyright © Steve Campbell 2011
All rights reserved, including the right to reproduce this
book, or any portions thereof, in any form.
This novel is a work of fiction. Any references to real people,
events, establishments, organizations or locales are intended
to give the fiction a sense of reality and authenticity.

Previously published in unedited form online at
http://theamericanapocalypse.blogspot.com.

Contact the author: stevcampbell@yahoo.com

First Paper Edition: July 2011

This story is based on a photograph of "Brian" by Tom Stone.

http://www.tomstonegallery.com/

The Lion

I like to sit here and watch the cars pass by. Maybe later I will go sit in front of where the Starbucks used to be. I do a lot of sitting. I am sitting on the edge of the Black Forest, that's what I call it, but I don't think it really has a name, I feel safe. No one, well hardly anyone comes by.

I don't like to talk to people. Nobody really knows that I don't like too either. Not that anyone cares. I hide it well. Why? It's because people scare me on so many different levels. I only realized a few days ago that I scare people too. That was such a surprise to me! I am not sure why I do. I know that I am homeless but I didn't think it was noticeable. Hell, being homeless is no longer that unusual. I mean I try not to smell, and my clothes, at least to me, seem okay. I am not a scary old bum with leather skin and barbed wire hair who reeks of booze or worse. I am just me. Whatever me is which isn't much by anyone's standards including my own. Maybe I radiate homeless rays? I wish I had someone I could ask.

I also wish I had money. I am hungry. If I move from where I am sitting anytime soon it will be because of the breeze. I am downwind of McDonald's and the wind is smelling good. McDonald's hasn't closed yet like most of the other stores in the shopping center and for that I am very glad. It would be harder for me to survive if they did.

McDonald's is the source of many things that are good in my life. Well, they were. Like everything and everywhere goodness seems to be decreasing. *"A shortage of goodness."* I say this to myself and smile. I am not sure why it is happening. A lot of things in life are like that you see. Stuff happens for no reason. People appear in my life than disappear. I don't even understand why I do so many of the things that I do so I guess it is no surprise that I don't understand why things happen like they do. Even my thoughts seem alien to me at times. There not as bad as the ghosts. I am not going to talk about the ghosts now. It might bring them and today I don't feel like seeing any if I can avoid it.

McDonald's is good for a lot of reasons. Maria and Anna sometimes save food for me depending on who the shift supervisor is. Also I usually find a used cup that I can take in for refills. When I do that I have to move quickly. I know the atmosphere changes inside when I come. That makes me uncomfortable. Also, sometimes the manager yells at me. He really shouldn't do that. They also moved all the ketchup and other stuff up by the counter. I used to take a cup and pump ketchup into it, add water, and pretend it was soup. I only do that when I am hard up and very hungry.

Sometimes I check the trash cans too. They don't have much in them that is worthwhile these days. I also have competition for the food in the cans now. I don't know what to do about that. I thought if I was nice maybe we could share the food. They didn't understand what I meant. They laughed at me so I left. What made it worse was Anna saw it through the window. They don't understand. If I still had my heart I would be different man. More brave and maybe even smarter. A hero. I have not been right since my mother stole in a fit of anger at me. She has disappeared, that was okay, but she took my heart with her and that isn't okay. I need it out here.

Anna waves to me from McDonald's. I wave back halfway. I say halfway because my hand drops and I turn away halfway through it. I am embarrassed. She saw me, the me that has no heart, fold in front of those two Tree People. She doesn't understand. They invoked the ghosts with their words that day. I didn't run from them. I ran from who they called. I know them. They know me those Tree People. They are Hurters and Hurters scare me. They scare me real bad. They smell my fear and know just like I smell the old pain from others that sticks to them. Their skin is washed in the tears of others and dried with the breath from their cries.

    "I don't know what to do. I don't know what to do"
loops in my head like a bad song. I need to move. To go
somewhere. Anywhere. I pull my hood up. I like my hood.
When it is up I feel invisible. I need to feel invisible now.

    I walk the long way. Instead of taking the path
through the woods I walk around them. Not because I am
scared. I just need to do it. I head towards the Lambs Center.
It is a Christian place. What else could it be with that name?
People go there and sit outside. They have a shower they let
people use during certain hours. I never get the hours right so
I never get to take a shower there. They also have two
washing machines and dryers. Usually only the washer
works. The dryer does but it takes forever to dry the clothes.
It is free and the list of people that want to use it is very long.
Sometimes I get lucky. They let me wash mine when I show
up and the person scheduled for that time doesn't. I am not
carrying anything much today. Just my daypack with a few
things in it that I don't want to take the chance on them being
stolen.

    My day pack is my life. I learned that the hard way. I
only carry things in there that are special to me. I don't have
many of them. I have lost too many day packs along the way
to keep anything. I once had a box. It was metal and was
painted with a picture of a girl and plants. I think, based on
the writing on it, that it once held tea. A girl gave it to me.
That made it very special. I lost it when I thought I had
hidden my pack in a safe place. I get to the Lamb Center and
I see a group of Hurters waiting out front. None of the people
I considered friends were there so I just kept on walking.
    There is a shopping center next to the center with a
restaurant that has the best smells coming from it. I have only
been inside once but I always like to walk on the sidewalk
next to the windows and look in at the people sitting in the
booths. The restaurant is called "Arties" and is very
expensive. It looks like it is and it sure smells like it. All the

wait staff are young, white, and good looking. For awhile it was a magical place to me. One time I got up the courage to go through the revolving door. That was fun! I wanted to go through it again but I knew that it would make people stare. I had gathered up my courage and decided I would apply for a job there. I thought about it for days and days before I actually did it.

In my mind by the last day of thinking about it I already had the job. I pictured myself smiling and taking orders from rich people. The one blond waitress I had seen a few times through the window would be helping me. We would fall in love and I would stay at her apartment which I knew was clean and had a soft bed with nice smelling sheets. We would be very happy.

So I went through the revolving door and was popped out in front of a desk with three women, all young and cute behind it. I was dizzy with excitement. They all said "Hello" and smiled but then their smiles got funny. They drooped an almost fell off their faces. Not quite though. If they had fallen off completely I probably would have run back out. I was excited, and since in my head I had convinced myself I had the job, I kept going.

"Can I help you?" This was from the one in the middle. She was tall. As tall as me and I am 6 feet tall. "I'm here for my job." I realized right away that didn't sound right. "I mean I am here to apply for my job." That still didn't sound right but I was getting nervous and people were standing around staring at me and more were coming in through the revolving door. I realized then it was dinner time.

I had forgotten that there was a dinner time and that restaurants got busy then. This was not at all how I pictured it happening in my head. I had the feeling it was slipping away but I was determined. The middle one said "Ah, you want to apply for a job..."

"Yes!" I leaped for like that a drowning man would for a life preserver someone safe on a boat casually tossed in his direction. She smiled. A thin lipped, smirky kind of smile, and reached underneath the desk they were all standing at. The girls that flanked her were grinning at each other like they had a secret giggle only they could taste. I knew that look. In the empty space where my heart should be I felt my light draining out of me. She lifted it and pointed it at me. Pointed it like a gun or a stake. I reached out to take it from her and time stopped.

Her hand, pale and clean. The nails had a soft gleam. The skin, it was perfect just like her. A skinny diamond sparkly bracelet that was impossibly elegant encircled the flesh and bone of her wrist. Then there was my hand moving towards her, stopping close enough that both were framed in a block of vision that was like a window. A window she had forgotten to close and now my hand had crept in uninvited.

My nails ripped and gnawed to the quick. Black grease creased along the skin. Grubby. Ugly. Me. It was like the entire world had stopped and focused on me and my ugly hand. I looked up and all three of the girls were staring at it. I slowly pulled my hand back. Their eyes followed it. No more smiles or secret shared giggles. I turned and ran. It only got worse. I tried to run out the revolving door but it had people coming in. I tried to squeeze into one of the slices of pie as they turned and scared some old lady plus it caught me and bit me. I heard the laughter as I tumbled out and onto the sidewalk. Buzzing laughter. The kind of laughter that meant Bad Things. I ran that day. I ran and ran and ran.

I ran that day like I had never run before. I was seriously sucking wind when I stopped. My side was starting to ache and I was hacking up Marlboro's from two years ago. Yet, as soon as I felt semi-recovered I was back to running. The pain, the pain stops pain. Sounds strange I know but it is one of my secrets. Some secrets you just can't tell people. I learned that early.

No one wants to believe Nice Mommy is really not so nice. "Stupid kid! Stupid kid! Can't be true cause you're a stupid lying kid" was part of the lyrics to my childhood song. Mommy would smile at them and casually mention, "Oh he is good boy but he ...." Here she would drop her voice down to sugarland and love levels and mention "The Doctor." When she was done, then they, they being who ever believed me or thought something wasn't quite right. They would give me that smile. The "I can't believe I thought, believed, wondered, such dark evil possibilities." The "such a nice kid for being so messed up" smile. After I saw that I knew I was doomed.

Pretty soon that smile went away. I was no longer young enough to be cute or troubled. I was just a pain in the ass, probably doing dope, lying, stupid no more a kid. Mommy... Oh Mommy. She brought the pain late at night. Bad Pain! Bad Pain! I ran and held my hands over my ears and screamed. Bad pain. So very, very bad.

That day, well, it was really night by the time I stopped running, I ended up under a tree. A big tree with nice chairs underneath. I sat in one and went right to sleep. When I woke up there was a guy about my age standing there under the tree watching me. I was lost for a second. Part of the bad thoughts and dreams still clung to me. Walking up in strange places is no big deal. What, at least for me, is crossing the border from where I go when I sleep to where I am when I wake up. Sometimes it is easy. Sometimes it's not so easy.

I stared at him and he stared at me. I think he knew something because he gave me time to get all my little shadow people thoughts together and across the border together in one group. Sometimes they stray off and I lose a few and I feel incomplete until I find them. When I felt like we had all made it I said "Hi."

He looked at me. I thought he was going to smile. Instead he said "Hey." Then we both stared at each other. It wasn't uncomfortable but I felt the need to explain why I was there. It wasn't my tree. Maybe it was his.

"I was sleeping."

"I noticed."

I checked him out. He wasn't staring at me which made it easier. He was just watching. He had lots of invisible eyes. I knew right away he was a Watcher, they are rare, but there was more. I just wasn't sure yet what. Then I noticed the gun. He was a cowboy! No, that couldn't be right. Well it could. I knew this, I sent a quick plea "Come on shadow thought people -- help me!" They did. I blurted "Gardener!"

He just stared at me. He wasn't surprised that I knew who he was. Then again if my world had a star he was one of them. Unlike the others whose fame came from their cruelty or connections. Him, and that other guy Max, they were known as fair but not to be fucked with. Some of us even slept at night in empty houses in the area that they had marked as "theirs" because it was safer. The freaks and drug crazed had learned not to cross their boundaries or them. Of course we couldn't stay. Come morning it was time to migrate back to where the action was or deal with getting moved on by them. Some people said he was crazy like that was bad or something.

"So what are you doing here." He said this flatly. I knew what he was really saying of course.

I bit back the first thing that came to mind. Besides I had already said it. Normally I would have smiled and told him I was just passing through. Then he would have said, "Make sure of it" or something like that. I would get up, say, "See ya," and start what I knew was going to be a long walk back to where I belonged. Instead, perhaps because of what happened, or maybe just because of who he was I decided not to. I had to tell someone. Maybe he would know.

"Do you have ghosts?" It sounds strange but I really thought he might understand. His eyes narrowed and I saw him evaluating me. Deciding how and if he was going to respond. Like a comic book I saw the balloons form and disappear over his head in rapid succession. Pop! Pop! Pop! They went so very fast but I didn't miss a one of them.

"I know ghosts...why?"

So I told him about the Tree People and how they had taken my food. How I applied for a job. How the ghosts of me that was once upon a time would come to me, stand there, look at me, cry and ask me for explanations. Then I took a deep breath and told him my secret. "They took my heart. They came with sharp knives to my bed. My Mother watched them and helped. She laughed when they opened my chest, took my heart, and put it in a white Styrofoam box and took it away. Now I have no heart! I can't be a hero or good anymore. They took it from me!" I was crying and I shouted the last part.

He didn't move. Didn't blink. Didn't look at me with one of those looks. He just said "They do that."

"He knew!" That was my first thought. My second, which I spoke out loud was, "How did you get your heart back?" I really wanted to know. He thought about, cocked his head a bit, and said "I dug for it." That confused me. I wanted to ask him more but he said "I guess you'll be going." Not much I could say to that. Plus I was still trying to figure out what the hell he meant. "Dig for it? Was there a secret burial place for Hero hearts? Were they stored somewhere?" I told him, "Yeah. I'm gone." Then I got up and started walking back to what I called home, the woods by McDonald's. I could feel his Watcher eyes on me every step of the way until I turned off on a bike path.

I looked around once I hit the path for a decent clump of bushes to take a leak behind. I had been wanting to go since my eyes had opened but I had to wait. Having a real bathroom not far from where I slept was one of the few things from my past life I missed. I hadn't been the only one to use these woods this way. Flies were buzzing around a couple piles of shit off to one side. Thank god I hadn't stepped in it. Just being me guaranteed a little extra space. Stepping in human shit would increase that space by a mile or so. I guess I could think of that has a mixed blessing I thought as I wandered back on to the trail.

It was fairly quiet out here since it was early. A jogger pack passed me. No one jogged alone anymore. Women didn't jog at all anymore on this trail unless they had men with them or were armed. I had gotten over how unreal to see joggers pounding by you with weapons strapped to their leg in one of those fancy military holsters. Now it was just one of those things.

While I walked I thought about what Gardener had told me. Jesus, I had a hard enough time figuring out what people meant normally. I was totally lost when they went cryptic. Yet he knew what I meant. "Dig up a heart. Dig up a heart." This kept going through my head. "Why would Gardener tell me to dig up my heart?" Then it hit me! I got a visual of Mrs. Montez digging in her flower beds with a trowel! Holy Shit! He was telling me to get a trowel! I was glad I figured it out. A lot of times I thought I had figured things out only to realize that I hadn't. When I was a kid in school my answers often made the other kids laugh and laugh. I didn't understand why. Later I learned to pretend that I was just being funny. I still knew who the joke was on - It just made it easier to play off. The problem was going to be finding a trowel. Then figuring out where to dig. I would just have to look for signs. Sometimes when I was in the woods I thought I saw things out of the corner of my eye. Maybe they were connected? It was possible.

I thought this over as I walked. No money was going to be a problem. Where could I get a free trowel? "Dummy!" I felt like smacking myself. I was walking down a street filled with houses. At least a third of them were empty. Empty houses often had good stuff left over from the people before. I just needed to find one with those little midget metal houses in the back. I searched my brain. I knew there was a name for them I just couldn't remember it. I hated this. So many things slipped away when I needed them. I often thought of my thoughts as fish. Big thoughts like this were big fish. Hard to hold on to and with a life of their own. They would dodge my hands as I tried to pull them in, hug them, and squeeze out what I needed. I never hurt them and always let them go. They never understood this and fought with me every single time. Stupid fish. All I could come up with was midget house, hot, and grass smelling place. I shrugged and forgot about it.

It was still early enough that no one was really up yet. Sometimes in developments like this where there were still a lot of people I would get yelled at by neighbors or they would tell me they were going to call the cops. I quit worrying about it awhile back when I realized that the cops never came and the people never left their yards. In fact, it had been awhile since anyone had yelled anything. I guess they were afraid. There were a lot of crazy people running around now.

I started looking for the tell tale signs. Empty houses may have their lawn cut and curtains still in the windows but I always knew when was empty. I could feel it. It felt like home. It felt like me. I turned off and began walking up the driveway of the first one I spotted. This one didn't have any windows to see into the garage. I figured the garage might be a good place to look too. I was pleased with myself. My brain was working pretty good today. That made me smile. It was a happy feeling. I went around back. Nothing except a broken bird bath. I tried the faucet. The way things were happening today I hoped I might get lucky and get some water. None. Oh well. It didn't surprise me. I was enough of a realist not to expect too many good things in one day.

I lost count of the houses I had checked after the third one. I did get some water. An old guy was in his back yard watering his garden next door to one of the houses I checked. I asked him if I could drink from his hose. He was undecided at first, I saw his hand go down and check that the gun he was carrying was still there in its holster. That reassured him enough that he came over to the chain link fence that I was on the other side of and tossed the hose over. I turned the little sprayer thing back on and drank as much as I could, maybe a little bit more. I was hungry too and eating water was filling. I told him, "Thanks!" but he didn't want to talk. When I tossed the hose back over the fence I thought he might say something. He looked like he wanted to but he didn't.

The next house I checked was where I found it. I knew then I was destined for something good. I am never usually this lucky so many times in one day.

I found it just in time. I was starting to get discouraged. All the goodness of the day was evaporating. One of the ghosts was knocking hard on the door in my head. I could hear her and I didn't want to let her in. She always got in anyways. Sometimes I would press my hands to my head to keep the door shut. She would knock on it to get my attention. It sounded like a woodpecker and it made my head hurt. The knocking would stop and I would hear her voice, the one I knew so well. She would tell me "You're a fuckup. Don't kid yourself. You're a fuckup. It's your fault. It's always your fault." I would yell at her, "Go away Mom!" Sometimes she wouldn't leave and I would start crying. She was so mean. I must be bad. Mom's always love their boys. She said so. It must be me. She is right. I am bad and a fuckup.

She was going to get through the door soon. I was going to have to hurry up and get back. Find somebody with something to drink. If I drank enough then it didn't bother me so much. Sometimes to get the money I would have to be a bad boy. That wasn't so bad most times except when they hurt me. Even then it was okay because I was a fuck up and deserved it. As long as I knew I could get free I was okay. No matter how bad I felt I never let them tie me up. Then I could get crushed. Crushed by their love. Crushed by monsters. Crushed by their oily snakeyness in me.

That's when I saw it. A midget metal house. Damn. I hoped this one didn't have spiders. I didn't like spiders and the last one had a lot of them. I just gritted my teeth and looked anyway. Heroes need hearts and I had to find one. If I had to deal with spiders then I would. When I got out of the last metal house without finding anything I felt like spiders were on me. Crawling up and down. Up and down. So I rolled in the grass. That was fun. I felt like a big dog until that made me itch too. I had grass stains on my clothes. It made for a good smell. A summer smell.

This little house was going to have to be a quick search. The door was squeaking and pecking. I had to go fast. I just stuck my head in and there it was! Just like someone had left it for me! A trowel! It wasn't alone either. It had friends. A claw looking thing and tiny little rake were next to it. Standing up nice and tall next to them was a shovel. It was a family! I said "Sorry" to them, and then I reached in, grabbed the trowel and ran. I don't know why. I just did.

I stopped. Running is tiring. Plus it gets boring sometimes. I hoped Father Shovel wouldn't mind me running off with his kid. He had another one. He probably wouldn't miss my trowel. I was getting closer to my woods, the Black Forest, the land of ghosts. So far real people had been scarce. Or least scarce enough that I felt alone most of the time. I didn't always sleep in the forest. Sometimes I slept at other peoples places. Not as often as I used to. It was like every year I got older the kindness of strangers, and the strange, receded. I felt old when I was nineteen.

I took the path off the road about a half mile before the McDonald's. It wasn't really a path as much as where trees had been cleared for a sewer line a long time ago. Maybe ten years or so. I don't know. Weird pipes stuck up in a few places and let out stinky air. There were raised concrete domeish things with metal manhole covers on top every once in a while. They were good for sitting on.

I kept some stuff in plastic bags that I hid under a fallen oak right off this path. The trash bags were black and once you threw some leaves and sticks on them they were invisible. So invisible that I couldn't find them one time when I was really drunk. I ended up sleeping on the ground and woke up freezing. It took me damn near a week to find them. Boy I was blowing snot for awhile after that.

I kept a tarp, well a part of a tarp, some blankets, a plastic flute that I was going to learn to play really well. I liked the flute. I pictured myself sitting in the woods playing it and making magic good ghosts come out. Maybe little green cookie elves that would bring me food. I also had some books and papers. One had a really cool design that someone had drawn. The other was a shopping list and a phone number. It was written by a woman. This I knew. I liked looking at it and imagining things. Little plays in my head. Plays that had her...she never had the same face as the star. Usually it was whoever I had seen in the parking lot or maybe going into McDonald's or getting gas.

She was always pretty with clean straight hair. She had a job doing something important. Not real important. Even in my dreams I knew not to go to far as to make then unbelievable to myself. Something good. A job where people said "Hi" to her and she went to meetings. I knew meetings were important. I had been to a few and my life always changed after a meeting.

She would have an apartment and I would have the list. I would be going shopping for us. I would bring it home and she would be waiting and happy. She would talk to me. It would be like cable TV except there wouldn't be badness. Sometimes I would be important too. I would have really nice sunglasses, my tooth wouldn't hurt, and no one could hurt me.

Instead of going by my place in the woods I decided to go to McDonald's and see if Ana or Marie could part with some food. I was hungry. As soon I decided to do that I got even hungrier. "Stupid stomach." I thought to myself as I stuck the trowel in my belt. It was kind of like a knife that way. "Armed and dangerous" I thought and laughed.

I was surprised when I got there to see Ana, Maria, and Tina the shift supervisor sitting outside at one of the round like a hamburger tables. They did not look happy. I kind of approached them at an angle. Just in case you know. Ana saw me, waved and yelled, "Hey Brian! Come sit with us!" No one else looked enthused about that idea but I didn't mind. I liked Ana. Mostly because she liked me. Her, and Maria, they always fed me when the bad shift supervisor wasn't around. I was hoping for an Angus Deluxe meal. Tina was okay with it too. I knew I would have to do some idle chit chat to get it. That part I wasn't looking forward to.

I walked up to them. I hated that they stared at me as I did too. It made me feel stiff. Ana was smiling. Maria, I noticed was crying silently. No wonder she didn't want to see me. Bad Things were happening. I could feel them.

Ana asked me as soon as I got close enough, "How are you Brian? Where you been?"

"Why is Maria crying?" was my reply.

Maria answered me, "Because Maria doesn't have a job anymore."

Ana said gently, "We're all gone. They closed this McDonald's." Now she was looking sad too. Tina, sitting at the next table snorted. I guess that meant something. I wasn't sure what.

I was dumbfounded. "But...but everyone eats here!" This was not good. "But I'm hungry!" God, I know I sounded like a baby as soon as I said that. Ana's face fell and Maria started to say something. It was going to be mean too. I could tell. Ana held up her hand and cut Maria off. "I know Brian. We're all going to know how that feels soon..." Ana stood up, stared defiantly at Tina and said "I'm getting us all food. If they don't like it well fuck 'em."Ana, over her shoulder, as she stomped away said, "Brian. Angus right?"

"Yep."

As soon as she disappeared through the employee door Maria started giving me a hard time. "You come around here sniffing for food. Boy, you are stupid aren't you." It wasn't a question. It was a statement. I thought "What the hell? Why is she attacking me? What did I do?" What I said was "Huh?"

"You know that girl likes your sorry homeless ass. Don't you?"

I said the first thing that came into my mind. "Why?" I heard Tina snort and then laugh. Tina was definitely a snorter. Maria stared at me, opened her mouth to say something, and then closed it. She waved her hand in the air and scattered cigarette ash on her smock. She didn't bother to brush it off either. "Never mind. Don't matter. She has bigger problems."

Tina, over at the next table chimed in "Yeah. Like a job." She muttered something to herself and crossed her arms.

We sat there in silence until Ana returned. I got my Angus! Everybody else got yogurt parfaits and double cheese burgers. Tina looked at hers, looked at Ana, and then tossed it over her shoulder. I made a mental note of where it landed for later. I told her, "Thanks Ana!" Then I dug in. I got about half way through when the Hurters arrived. As soon as I saw them come around the corner I wanted to stuff the rest of my Angus burger in my day pack. The only reason I didn't was it was too late.

Shit. My luck sucked. It was the Hurter twins. They weren't twins. They didn't even look the same. I still saw them as twins in my head. They went everywhere together and every where they went no one wanted them to come back. Ana said under her breath "Shit. It's Beevis and Butthead." I laughed. That was pretty good. My timing could have been better.

The big one said "What's so funny dickhead?" His partner, Shorty, he was short too, chimed in, just as I knew he would with "You laughing at us?" I was getting a sick feeling in my tummy. I knew where this was going because I had been there before. I was right. It wasn't good at all.

"Great. I'll take that." Then the Big Hurter bent over and snatched my half finished Angus! I yelled "Hey! Give it back!" as I tried to get untangled from the stupid table seat. That's when he hit me in the chest. I fell, bounced off the table and fell sideways. As I did I felt something in my leg give. That hurt more than the punch. A lot more. I heard laughter, and the Little Hurter, Shorty, say "Get them yogurts too. I be liking my yogurt."

I rolled off the seat and hit the ground. It was dirty down here. I thought "Maybe I should stay down here. Maybe even crawl under the table where it would be harder to get me. I had a Hurter take his boots to me before. I didn't want it to happen again. In the background I heard the others yelling. Ana ripped something off in Spanish. I didn't need to a translator to know she had just called them queers. I knew that word. Then I heard the smack of a hand on flesh, a scream, and Ana had joined me on the concrete. I looked across at her. We looked at each other and I didn't miss what her eyes were telling me. I wanted to scream at her "I don't care! I'm not a hero! I don't have a heart!" Then I heard Shorty say "Drag the bitch back up here and bend her over. I'll show her whose a *maricón.*

There was bad coldness in his voice. I saw Big Hurters arms come down, pick her up, and watched as she tried to fight lose. In the background Tina yelled "I'm calling 911!" Shorty laughed and said "Go ahead. They don't come anymore."

"Oh god please help me" I prayed. I wanted to hide. They were going to crush her. Ana cried out "Brian!" and started sobbing. This wasn't right. Crushing is bad! Bad! I rolled out from under the table and tried not to scream from the pain in my leg. I looked up. The Hurters were busy. Shorty was trying to get Ana's pants down. Maria was just standing there and I couldn't see Tina. A little voice said "Don't let them do this Brian. If you do you will go far away and never come back." I pushed myself up. "What the hell did I have to stop them?" Then I remembered the trowel. I pulled it out and said "Hey!" I had to say it twice to get their attention.

Shorty stopped, looked over his shoulder and laughed. "You're pathetic." Big Hurter grinned at me. I looked at my trowel. It was pathetic. A wooden handle with a steel curved scooper thing at the end. It even had dried dirt on it from the last person who used it. Shorty turned away and went back to paying attention to Ana's pants. Big Hurter reached under Ana and grabbed her breast and twisted it. He told her "Quit struggling until we're in bitch." Shorty had her pants halfway down. Ana needed to wash her underwear or buy some new ones. I was going to throw the trowel away and see how far I could get before they noticed I was gone when the same little voice said "Excalibur." Just like that. Then I remembered! The Sword in the Stone! I knew what I had to do! I had the answer!

I stepped forward, that hurt, raised the trowel, and drove it into Shorty's back. He had assumed the hunch position and was fumbling with his pants. I didn't drive it into him. I had gone for the center and hit something hard. I think it was bone. So I raised it up above my head and did it again. That went in a little deeper. I liked that. He was screaming louder than me an Ana combined. He sounded like a little girl. I grinned. Then Big Hurter was on me. I looked at him and my Mr. Smile froze. That's when he sunk that sheath knife he wore into me. I thought "*Why Big Hurter?*" When I looked into his eyes I got my answer. It was the same reply I had always gotten from Hurters. It said "Because I can." Then he pulled it out and hit me again. This was past hurt. I felt myself going down. "*No yogurt parfait for me today*" I thought and then I was back on the dirty concrete. I put my hands to where it hurt and knew I had dropped the trowel. That was stupid but I was leaking. Leaking blood.

Shorty was still howling. I looked up at Big Hurter. He looked at me puzzled. That was funny. What was he puzzled about? I heard Tina yell "Run you fucks! I called 911 and told them there's gunshots and a Officer was hurt!" Tina was a bitch but she wasn't stupid. That was about the only thing you could say that would get a response nowadays. Shorty was screaming "Help me!"

"Funny" I thought "He's still hunched over but there is no Ana now. Where's Ana?" I must have gone to sleep for a second because when I opened my eyes the Hurters were gone and my head was in Ana's lap. That was nice of her.

She was going to get her clothes messed up because I was leaking badly. It was even coming out my mouth. I knew that taste. I told her "Sorry...sorry Ana." I was sorry too. Sorry for so many things. So very, very many things. Her eyes were big and pretty. I never noticed that before. I tried to tell her what I wanted to tell her under the table. "Ana..."

"Ssshhhh."

I tried again. This was important. "Ana...I don't have a heart."

She smiled and said "Yes you do. You are Brian. Brian the Lion Heart...Don't you hear it?" She put her hand over mine where I was leaking so much. "I hear it mi amor." She heard it? I listened. She was right! I did have one! It was pumping so loudly now! Like a drum and it was tiring me out too...

1224183R00084

Made in the USA
San Bernardino, CA
01 December 2012